THANKFUL

A HOLIDAY ROMANCE

MICHELLE LOVE

HOT AND STEAMY ROMANCE

CONTENTS

Sign Up to Receive Free Books	v
Blurb	vii
1. Karin	1
2. James	17
3. Karin	28
4. Karin	38
5. James	46
6. Karin	54
7. Karin	62
8. Karin	70
9. James	79
10. Karin	86
11. James	97
12. Karin	105
13. James	113
14. Karin	120
15. Karin	127
Sign Up to Receive Free Books	131
Preview of On the Run	133
Chapter 1	136
Chapter 2	141
Chapter 3	146
Chapter 4	151
Chapter 5	156
Other Books By This Author	162
About the Author	165

Made in "The United States" by:

Michelle Love

© Copyright 2020 – Michelle Love

ISBN: 978-1-64808-126-2

ALL RIGHTS RESERVED. No part of this publication may be reproduced or transmitted in any form whatsoever, electronic, or mechanical, including photocopying, recording, or by any informational storage or retrieval system without express written, dated and signed permission from the author

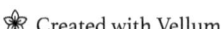 Created with Vellum

SIGN UP TO RECEIVE FREE BOOKS

Sign Up to Receive Free E-Books and Audiobook Codes.

Would you like to read **The Unexpected Nanny, Dirty Little Virgin** and **other romance books** for **free**?

You can sign up to receive these free e-books and audiobooks by typing this link into your browser:

https://www.steamyromance.info/free-books-and-audiobooks-hot-and-steamy/

Or this one:

https://www.steamyromance.info/the-unexpected-nanny-free/

BLURB

karin's miserable, dead-end relationship to a sexually neglectful, verbally abusive man drives her to confront him one Thanksgiving in front of guests. His dapper, seductive cousin suggests revenge sex. She resists, wanting to properly end her relationship, and he is supportive. Except, when her breakup attempt ends in a physical confrontation, the cousin intervenes and helps her. They start a hot affair—but her new lover has a secret: he's a jewel thief planning his next heist. When she finds out he got her pregnant, she runs away to protect their child from his dangerous allies. However, the cronies believe she might rat everyone out, so they want to hunt her down, forcing him to choose between them and her.

Karin: James is the cure for my dead-end se* life.

He's been after me since learning I am miserable with Terry, my dim-witted boyfriend.
I try to do the right thing, and refuse James until I'm single.

However, breaking up with Terry goes to hell fast when he gets violent.
Out of the blue, James defends me from Terry and we get away.
That night, he gives me a taste of everything in sex that I've been missing.
Naturally, I run away with him.
Goodbye, Terry; hello, James.

But James has a secret of his own: all the money he earns doesn't come from a usual occupation.
I could deal with the fact that he's a professional jewel thief—but his crew scares me.
When I learn I'm pregnant, he spills everything—and they are not happy.
The confrontation terrifies me. I'm leaving for my safety and the safety of our baby.

His partners are after me now; they don't think I'll keep my mouth shut.
When the posse tracks me down, will James choose his buddies … or us?

James: A charming little lady like Karin is too good for my foolish cousin.

Accordingly, I steal her. That's what I do.
Such an adorable submissive she is. What a gem.
I'd love to keep her and train her properly.
Unfortunately, my partners in crime, Dale and Andrew, are getting in the way.
They sense we can't trust her. They think she makes me weak.

I know they're to blame when she vanishes after a confrontation.

Nevertheless, I can't let go of her. She's everything I want in a woman ... and she's carrying my child.
At the least, I have to make sure they're both taken care of. I'm a burglar—not a deadbeat.
Worse, the guys are already after her. They're positive she'll turn us in.
I know they mean damage. If I get in the way, they'll turn on me too.

I don't give a damn. I'll kick both their asses if I have to.
Even if Karin wants nothing to do with me anymore, I can't let them hurt her—or our baby.

1

KARIN

Happy Thanksgiving! Hope you're having a great day! Please excuse me while I wash down some painkillers with my wine.

I'm so exhausted from cooking! A turkey with trimmings, green bean and mushroom casserole, salad, a pumpkin pie, and an apple pizza. My creations, and at my expense. I was cooking and cleaning the entire day, and cooking some more; all accomplished in the kitchen of my tiny apartment.

The trash is out; my studio is spotless. Five guests pack my secondhand dining table as I finally settle down to eat as well. Thank God, it's done, I reflect with a sigh, my feet aching as much as my head after all the effort.

I give my companions a smile. "This is the last dish, my friends. Thanks for waiting!"

At least I have a sense of accomplishment to ease my exhaustion and frustration. My place looks great. Mostly because I spent time scrubbing it and picking up empty beer cans and dirty plates. With its Impressionist prints and soft lavender walls, it looks good enough for entertaining, even if petite.

I'm determined to enjoy it as much as I can—but that might be difficult.

My boyfriend Terry is drunk at the dinner table for the fifth holiday in a row. He's been here all day, taking up my couch and making more clutter for me to clean up. His only contribution to Thanksgiving dinner has been three six-packs of watery lager, two of which he's already sucked down by himself.

His only interaction with me today, longer than "get me a sandwich," was his complaint when I was too busy to have a quickie before the guests arrived.

His floppy, unkempt reddish curls hide his sullen little black eyes as he hunches over his plate. He's been quiet and resentful since I pointed out taking some of the workload would give me time to ... help, as he calls it, before the guests showed up.

(You gonna help or what? That's the mating call of Terry Branham).

The logic escaped him—or he was too lazy. Apparently, even sex isn't worth stuffing a turkey or washing dishes to old Terry. No wonder he still lives with his mother.

As I watch him shoveling food into his mouth while occasionally giving me a morose glance, I feel myself quietly, finally, reach the end of my patience. I'm not even sad about it. It's more a sense of resignation—even relief.

You know what? It's been eighteen months of negotiating, reasoning, warning, imposing consequences, and getting nowhere with this immature, jobless, whiny drunk. I'm not a martyr. I'm done.

Tonight, after the guests go home, I'll tell him. It's better to spend Christmas alone than let him fuck up another holiday.

I will probably spend it alone, or nearly. Most of the guests are his family members, since I'm not in contact with mine—except for my sister, who sits next to me, insistently loading my plate. She barely came into town, or I would have had my backup for cooking earlier.

Samantha is everything I've never managed to be. She's a successful painter with her own gallery in San Francisco, she has a family waiting back there for her, and she's confident and beautiful. Elegant, stylish, and tall, she looks like a model in her dark, trim suit, her blonde hair straightened and dyed platinum to bring out our family's blue-green eyes. Meanwhile, here I am, barely managing to tame my tawny curls into a messy up-do, dressed in secondhand green velvet that I altered myself.

"Great spread, sis," Samantha says with a rakish smile. "Now get some food in your stomach. You must be wiped after working all day with no help."

"I agree, this is quite delicious," another voice comments from the other end of the table. It's smooth and cultured, with just that touch of the Carolinas to always make my toes curl. Same goes for the man speaking them.

"My compliments," continues Terry's cousin with a slow smile, his chocolate-colored eyes twinkling. And suddenly half of my exhaustion is forgotten.

Time stops for a moment and I catch my breath as his warm, gentle gaze holds mine hypnotically. His name is James Beaumont, and he's such an amazing dish. I can't believe he shares any genes with Terry. And I've never wanted to fuck anyone more.

I met him last Thanksgiving at Terry's mother's ramshackle bungalow, while we were choking down dry turkey and some mess of orange goop and marshmallows she called sweet potatoes. She spent the whole meal whining about how tough it was to achieve by herself, with her son and husband sourly devouring the results. Already somewhat nauseated by the bad food, and sympathetic to anyone who dealt with two Terries, I offered to cook next year.

After supper, the incredibly hot guy with razor-cut auburn hair and amazing eyes slipped up to me, not one drop of gravy on his bespoke charcoal suit. He stood out among his relatives like a gold watch gleaming in a weedy yard. One look in his eyes, and I forgot Terry was four feet away.

He introduced himself as James, Terry's cousin, and quietly thanked me for taking the duty next year. I invited him along with the others, of course, and was happier than I should have been when he agreed. I spent half the night talking to him—and had sizzling dreams about him every night for over a week afterward.

"Thanks," I say shyly, and his lips quirk.

"Yeah, thanks for making good on your promise. It's not like I can get that from either of these two." Terry's mother, Caroline, is heavyset and tiredly pretty, with the same russet curls as her son.

His father is an older version of him, aside from his hair being straight, thin and gray-blond. The son glares; the father just keeps shoving food into his mouth as if he's at a four-star buffet. I'm not sure if he's hard of hearing or just doesn't give a shit. Maybe he's just this desperate for real food.

"Don't you be a bitch too, Mom. I'm already getting that from my so-called girlfriend," Terry growls angrily, glaring daggers at me.

OH FUCK. Now what? Is he drunk enough to bring up our relationship in front of his mother? If he does, I'm not showing him any mercy.

"WHAT DID SHE DO, ask you to wash a dish?" And then his

mother and Terry are off bickering at each other, while I try to focus on eating.

SAMANTHA SCOFFS. "Why I married a chick, in a nutshell," she mutters in my ear.

I give her a tight, rueful smile. Samantha is bi and doesn't seem to fully grasp sometimes what it's like to only want men. She also likes to forget that women can be awful too, since she married a good one.

"YEAH," I sigh back, a moment before draining my wineglass. I reach for the bottle to get a refill as Terry's mom rips into him about his hygiene. "I'm done."

SHE LOOKS RELIEVED. "GOOD." And just like that, she's on to something more pleasant, trying to distract me. "So how's the latest decorating project?"

I STOP AT HALF a glass and set the bottle down. "I made rent and bills with it." Barely. How I wish that I was rich.

THAT MAKES me glance over at James again, sitting there exuding class and money, like he doesn't belong with the rest of his kin. He's calmly trying to defuse the argument, though he comes down solidly on Mom's side. Thanks, James. At least someone in that family prefers reason to arguing.

. . .

I wonder how awkward these gatherings are for him, having to deal with people acting so ... beneath him. He always seems so calm and poised, like nothing rattles him. I wish I knew his secret.

"Small potatoes again, huh? What was it this time, another baby room?" Samantha shakes her head and lays a hand on my shoulder.

"A preschool. She just didn't have much money." I'm young and hungry for work, and Annabelle was a good client.

"You gotta stop selling yourself short, honey. You're never gonna get out of student loan debt taking small jobs." She looks over at Terry in annoyance. "Hey! It's fucking Thanksgiving. Quit bitching at your poor mom."

I tense up at once: one of my million problems with Terry is his temper. But then I think, what the hell does it matter? I'm breaking up with him anyway.

He immediately glares at Samantha. "Mind your own business."

"I'd love to, but you're too damn loud for anyone to avoid your fucking business." She gives him an overly sweet grin and he turns a few shades redder.

. . .

"I don't have to put up with—" he starts—and his mother slaps her hand against the tabletop hard enough to shake it.

"Terry! You don't get to mooch your whole life and then complain when people point it out. Now shut up and let's eat!"

I'm glad for the backup—but it's too late. Terry has had too much beer, and the fury in him wants to make a mess of things. "You started it," he snaps. "And now I'm angry!"

"Dear God," Samantha sighs. "Nobody cares, Terry—"

"Oh shut up, you man-hating bitch!" Terry splutters—and it humiliates me. So much that I go from I'm breaking up with him all the way to what the hell did I ever see in this bozo?

There are a million reasons, but what it boils down to is the same damn thing Samantha was poking at me about. I settle for too little. And I don't care enough about how it hurts me until it affects someone close to me.

But now it has—and I was pissed to begin with.

"You watch your goddamn mouth when you're talking to my sister," I hiss—and Terry freezes. I've never been anything but kind and firm with this man-baby—probably kinder than I should have been. But you don't fucking insult the one person in my family that still talks to me.

"Babe, what's ... gotten into you?" he asks in a deeply worried voice as I stand up.

"You," I reply, as everyone goes quiet. I can feel the room hold its breath. Samantha looks like she's gleefully anticipating a total bloodletting of this fucker's ego, and I know why.

There are consequences once I'm past my limit. And Terry just rocketed past it and kept right on going.

"You've gotten into me, Terry. I told you what would happen if you messed up another holiday with me." I stare at him coldly while all the color drains from his weak-chinned face.

"Wait, come on. I helped! I brought beer! I—" He's blinking at me in blank horror, as if a pod person has replaced his sweet, patient girlfriend. The sweet, patient girlfriend who already warned him that she was running out of patience with him.

"Let us eat our food in peace," I growl, still staring unblinkingly into his eyes as he wilts faintly. Next to me, Samantha chokes on her wine.

. . .

He stares back at me nervously, then grabs his fork and stuffs a bite of food in his mouth. He's already muttering rebelliously under his breath but that's a lot easier to ignore. For now, anyway.

"So, you're an interior decorator?" James asks, catching my eye again. I feel warmth run through me and nod silently. "I might have a job or two for you that would be higher-end. I'll be happy to discuss it with you after supper."

The good, juicy turkey I've roasted turns to sand in my mouth. I swallow with a great effort and nod, and the corners of his eyes crinkle with amusement.

"Good. Don't let me forget, now," he says, with an almost gleeful tone. Out of the corner of my eye, I can see Terry watching us; James notices it as well and looks even more amused.

I catch my breath, feeling like I'm on the brink of something. It should scare me, but instead, I find myself excited. What is this man offering me besides a job?

I've never really wanted a normal life. I've always wanted to be part of something extraordinary. Some kind of adventure.

Maybe even a wild affair.

. . .

But instead I've ended up settling for what I can get, time and again. Low-paying jobs; guys like Terry.

One look at James, and I suddenly want to take crazy risks, visit exotic places, and drink wine costing my entire paycheck for a single glass.

Sitting across the table, Terry stares at us with increasing intensity. He misses everything—including my growing unhappiness with him. Unexpectedly, I'm talking to another man about a totally neutral subject, and he's laser focused on it.

Another charming habit of Terry's: he does very little to keep me, yet he's still horribly jealous. It's another way he exhausts my patience—and I have none left. Samantha pokes me gently in encouragement, and I finally smile.

"I'd love to trade up to a better ..." Man. Are you single? "... paying class of clientele."

His smile vaguely broadens. "Lovely."

"Oh, for fuck's sake!" Terry explodes, jumping from his seat and leaning aggressively over me. "Are you gonna hit on my cousin right in front of me?"

"What the hell are you talking about?" his mother snaps

incredulously. "She didn't do a thing! They were talking business! What, are you jealous of James now?"

"Who the hell wouldn't be, the rich prick? Bad enough you drag him around to every family gathering like he's your son instead of your sister's!"

My eyes widen as I look between them. James is wincing and covering half his face. Samantha is chomping away at her food like it's a bucket of popcorn and she's got good seats at a midnight movie showing. Terry's dad is going for thirds.

"I warned you twice, Terry," I say in a low, hard voice. This is it. In my life I have never been more elated than deciding not to give boyfriends my apartment key after the first break-in.

"Warned me? Warned me what, whore? You were so busy with all this stupid cooking, you wouldn't even get me off today!" He's on a full-blown rant, blissfully unaware that he's sawing the floor out from under himself.

I stare at him as he splutters on, agitated. "You frigid bitch, you know it wouldn't have even taken you two minutes—"

Silence descends upon the table with a grave heaviness. Terry's father drops his fork onto the table with a clatter. His mother stares at her son wide-eyed, lips trembling.

. . .

James has a coughing fit; his handsome face flushes, tears gathering at the corners of his eyes.

Terry's mug slowly goes from purple to white as it dawns on him what he just said in front of God, his parents, and the rest of us. In that same moment, as the instant regret takes over, Samantha loses it completely and nearly falls out of her chair laughing.

I observe Terry, considering the way he's left his well-deserving ass wide open, and say in a cold voice, "You said it. I didn't. But after tonight, it's not my dilemma anymore."

"What the fuck are you saying?" he demands. His whiny, defensive, baby-needs-a-nap tone sets my teeth on edge.

James sighs heavily. "Cousin, if you want a prayer of saving your relationship, or any degree of face, you should quit now."

Terry's head snaps around, his dull black eyes turning to slits. For one precious moment, it seems like he's going to restrain himself.

Instead, he opts to really wreck things. He grabs the edge of the table and literally tries to flip it onto me while we're all seated and in the middle of Turkey Day dinner. "Fuck you!" he yells, inflamed as he struggles to lift one end.

"Hey, knock it the hell off!" I yell at him. His mother is swearing at him; even his father joins as his overfilled plate spills over. Terry shakes his head like a stubborn kid; his face sweaty, eyes tightly shut, and teeth clenched. He tries again, letting out a feeble grunt of effort.

That's when I realize that someone else is holding the table down far more firmly than Terry can lift: James, with a frigidly annoyed look on his face. "You're spilling my wine," he warns his cousin.

"That's it!" I stand up and walk over to Terry. "We're done. Get the fuck out of my apartment."

That stops him cold; he blinks at me, as if shocked his attempt to bulldoze a Thanksgiving dinner in the middle of a tantrum has consequences. "But you're so charming! You can't just throw me out!"

"Well, I sure as hell can," his mother growls, getting up and pulling his battered blue puffer jacket out of the closet and throwing it at him. "You're embarrassing the crap out of me. Go wait in the goddamn car or you won't have a home to come back to."

. . .

Terry looks around at us, drunken puzzlement on his face, wondering why we're picking on him. Then he slowly takes the coat and turns to the door.

Once he slumps out, she sighs and smiles at me apologetically. "I'm sorry he's such a brat. Discipline has always been a problem for him." She cuts her gaze toward her husband, who is scooping food into his mouth once more.

I take a deep breath and force a smile at her. "Let's just finish this feast," I suggest softly. "He's an adult, and accountable for his own actions."

And the only goddamned reason I'm not calling you out for spoiling him silly is I'm handing his ass back to you. No more free babysitting. That's punishment enough for you.

At least with Terry brooding in the car like a banished kid, we can have our pie in peace. There's even some small talk; though it goes on around me, I struggle through my meal. My fatigue is tinged with sadness: not for ridding myself of Terry, but because it seems like I always have to choose between settling for guys like him, or being alone.

Although ... maybe not, I wistfully peek in James' direction. I'm surprised to see him looking at me with concern. When our eyes meet, I feel a thread of warmth and wonder for a moment if I'm the only one feeling it.

After dinner, Terry's parents take half of both of the pies without asking, wish me a happy Thanksgiving, and make themselves scarce. James sticks around, saying he'll take a cab, and helps Samantha and me clean up and pack the rest of the food.

"Okay, I have to admit, even if I didn't want to get away from everybody else over the holidays, I am definitely glad I came tonight." Samantha's normally perfect mascara is smeared at the corners from tears of laughter. "You okay after all of that?"

"Yeah, I'm just ... really tired." And disheartened. And embarrassed. But most of all, I'm bracing myself for the Breakup Talk that will happen tomorrow.

Terry probably won't even remember he was kicked out tonight, let alone the fact I said I'm done. I need to spell it out for him, and whether it's another goddamn temper tantrum ... Fuck it; I'll do it over the phone in case he starts breaking things again.

Once the table is cleared and everything is stored away, Samantha sighs and gives me a smile. "All right. Look, I've been on the road since four a.m. my time and I need to get some sleep. We still on for movies tomorrow?"

I nod at her and we hug goodbye. "Three o'clock. I'll pick you up at the hotel."

. . .

"Good." She looks between me and James, who is putting away the last of the dry dishes. "Looks like you have someone you should be talking to ... alone ... anyway."

She winks and gives me another hug, then breezes out, leaving blushing me behind her.

2
JAMES

I just watched Terry fuck up what will probably be his one chance to end up with a girl who is too good for him. I have to admit, it was pretty damn funny. But it's given the lovely lady in question an obvious headache, and that's not amusing at all.

Terry's been a burden on his mom for years, and he's always avoided growing up. He keeps searching for a nice girl who will take over Mom's babysitting duties, so he can mooch and drink and play video games while she does all the work, and it keeps failing. Then he blames the women for having backbones, instead of him having none.

It would be one thing if he was just a sad sack with no dick game; unfortunately, he's also a jerk with a violent streak. And I'm wary of what he might do next.

Growing up, I spent a lot of time with his family and he's the exact same guy now that he was at ten. And that's part of the reason I'm sticking around. Because once it finally dawns on this jackass that he's been dumped again, he'll lose it at sweet, sexy Karin—and he will not be calm about it.

When we were teenagers, I watched his dumb ass fail with women dozens of times. After Mom and Dad died, I lived in his house so many times that I ended up his sorta-brother, sorta-babysitter. From fourteen years old and on, he aggressively chased girls, got rejected—or had one give him a chance, only to blow it—and got malicious afterward.

Sometimes violently cruel. Once, I had to gather bail money for the little shit. The second time he got arrested, the family agreed to let him sit in jail for a few weeks.

I don't trust Terry will not come back tonight, once he drinks some more and works up some steam. He's done it twice before, and I won't let him try the same shit with this adorable, curly-haired girl I'm sitting across the couch from.

"Are you absolutely certain that you're doing all right?" I ask very gently. I've produced my flask of good brandy and a joint, and we're splitting them both. I draw on the joint and pass it over, lifting an eyebrow at her.

Karin looks at me with those dazzling, jewel-colored eyes and smiles thinly. "I will. I kind of saw this coming. Thanks for the weed; I might even be able to sleep." And she takes a tiny hit, like a nip.

"No problem. If sleeping is what you want to do, that is." Of course, there's another reason I've stuck around, besides making sure there's no confrontation, and that is Karin herself.

I've been attracted to her since the first time we met, in that primal, near-immediate way that has only hit me a few times with a woman. She has a sweet personality, a tight little body, and an ache that Terry just hasn't been satisfying, and I'm sure a lot of her needs he has not fulfilled.

I want to fix it. Badly. If she's been dealing with Terry this whole time, she has to be desperately in need of a proper fuck. I can provide that ... in fact, I'd be delighted to.

She'll be delighted, too ... if she's not too exhausted by the whole mess this evening, of course.

"I, um ..." It seems to be dawning on her what I'm suggesting; her cheeks turn endearingly pink. "Did you have some other idea?"

For a moment, I smile broadly, and her blush deepens. Adorable. "I imagine you're very unhappy with your soon-to-be ex-boyfriend," I purr at her. "And I really like you. Always have."

· · ·

HER EYES WIDEN A LITTLE, like she's waiting for me to say that I'm joking, or testing her, or something other than genuinely wanting to fuck her brains out. "Do you mean that you ..."

"I'LL BE BLUNT," I reply in a gentle tone. "I want to spend a few hours making you forget about my stupid cousin, who doesn't deserve you. I have a nice hotel room ten blocks away that we could go to."

SHE DRAWS A LONG, shuddering breath and her eyes dilate. She wants it; wants me. But then ... she surprises me.

"I SHOULDN'T GO SLEEPING with anyone else until I properly breakup with Terry," she admits with a sigh. "Otherwise I'd be grabbing my purse to go with you right now."

I'M SUDDENLY hard as a rock. A delayed yes is still a yes, even if I have to wait until she deals with the last of my cousin's drama. I take another swallow of brandy and smile at her.

"WELL, I'm not about to challenge you for being ethical. It's just another thing to like about you." My smile goes lazy. "Raincheck for tomorrow evening?"

SHE SQUEEZES her knees together and her lips part slightly with desire. She nods. "Make it nine tomorrow night."

. . .

"Nine it is. I'll bring dinner." I frown. I should tell her about Terry's violent responses to rejection.

"What is it?" she asks, looking a little worried.

"Terry. He's ..." Don't scare her needlessly. "... not known for taking breakups well. He doesn't have your key, does he? Or know where the spare is?"

She swallows and then shakes her head. "I never gave him one."

I go over to the street-facing windows: both are barred and locked. "Good. Are you planning on going out tonight?"

"Just to take the trash." She glances at the overfull bin behind her.

"Try to leave it for the morning if you can. Take your phone along if you can't."

She seems upset. "How much trouble should I expect?"

"If he shows up, chances are he'll be drunk and obnoxious. But tonight, don't go outside your door more than you need to and don't leave it unlocked when you take out the trash. If he shows up, don't open the door." I give her a wry look. "Call the number on that card I gave you and I'll shove a boot up his ass."

SHE GIGGLES. "You don't sound like you'd mind too much."

"I DON'T LIKE how he treats you, plain and simple. You deserve better than what he can provide." I turn back and approach her again as she gets up, pinch out the joint, and hand her the rest.

"I CAN DELIVER IT. However, if you want to give that fool his marching orders first, well ... as I said." I wink at her, and she smiles a touch wider. "I should really get going."

SHE FETCHES my good wool topcoat and helps me into it, a shy attempt at contact. "So ... nine o'clock tomorrow, then?"

I TURN and deliberately sever the touch barrier, caressing her cheek with two fingers. The shiver of anticipation running through her stiffens my cock again ... but she's made her choice, and I respect it. "See you then."

KARIN'S APARTMENT is on the third floor of a six-story brick walk-up with battered iron railings. My groin aches as I trot down the stairs with a dozen ideas of what to do to divine Karin tomorrow rolling through my head. I can't decide.

. . .

WE MAY HAVE to try a few things before the night is over.

TOMORROW NIGHT. Brilliant. Better if it happened tonight, but for a lovely lady like Karin, I don't mind waiting.

I LOOK UP and down the darkened street before taking my phone out to summon a ride. Too many cars, too many bushes, too many dark alleyways. A thief or another criminal—or a furious drunken boyfriend, about to be exed—could hide anywhere around here. I frown.

I HAVE THIS PECULIAR FEELING. I should test it before I depart for the night.

A MAN in my line of work lives by his instincts. I tell everyone who asks that I install security systems. Truth be told, I spend most of my nights at work deactivating them.

ESPECIALLY THE FANCY ones that guard wealthy people's gem collections.

NO ONE in my family knows I'm a professional thief. Families like ours, it's either incredible luck or crime to pull you out of poverty. I did not wait for luck, but I also have never been caught.

. . .

INSTINCTS ARE a big part of that. And right now, I smell a problem brewing.

SOMETHING CAUSES me to pause from calling a cab. Instead, I follow my hunch and saunter around the block. I hope I'm wrong ... but I'm not wrong very often.

BY THE TIME I round the last corner, my suspicions are confirmed; I hear an argument at Karin's place. I pick up my pace, careful on the icy pavement, and soon enough, Terry's voice is cracking with outrage.

"YOU CAN'T LEAVE ME! I won't fucking let you! Now let me in; we're having makeup sex right now!"

This is so much more cringe-worthy than usual. I break into a run. He sounds threatening—and he isn't taking no for an answer.

I HEAR Karin snap something back and he bellows "Shut up, whore!" and then a struggle begins.

"LET GO OF ME!" Karin screams. "Get out of the doorway! You can't come in! Go away!"

"OH, I'M COMING IN," Terry pants as I take the stairs to the third floor, two at a time. "I'm coming in and you're gonna make this up to me, or I'm gonna make you sorry!"

. . .

"Go fuck yourself! I said we're done!" A note of panic in Karin's voice fills me with rage. "Help!"

Of course, none of her neighbors respond. A few lights go on, but nobody comes out. New Yorkers in a nutshell: apathy is everywhere.

"I say when we're done, slut! I'm the man!" Terry yells, and then yelps to the sound of a hard slap.

"Well, you definitely are a piss-poor excuse for one," I remark in an icy voice once I'm directly behind him.

Terry freezes. His furry hand is still wrapped around Karin's wrist but he loosens his grip and she yanks it free.

I don't give him time to turn around; instead I grab him by the hair and the back of his shirt and pry him off the doorway. He yelps again, whining in protest as I slam him against the railing to cow him before taking hold of him again.

"I'm not bailing out your bitch ass any longer because you can't handle the consequences when you fuck up with women," I hiss in his ear as Karin watches us. "You can do one of two things.

You can leave down the stairs, or you can be a nuisance and get pitched over the railing."

"You just want her for yourself, you goddamn poacher! I'm not gonna be your cuck!" His voice is high with fear. I roll my eyes and pull his hair backward until he threatens to unbalance.

"You can't be a cuckold if you're no longer someone's boyfriend, you idiot. She's dumped you twice tonight. Denial doesn't change the damned facts."

I step up in front of him and give him a shake, staring into his eyes. "Now, are you going to leave, or are you going to land in the bushes and pick rose thorns out of your ass for the next three hours?"

He opens his mouth wide and closes it a few times, like a goldfish scooped up in a net. His anger has been replaced by raw panic. "Don't toss me over! It's a two-story drop!"

"Then get out of here." I shift my grip and give him a shove toward the stairs; he almost tumbles down headfirst before grabbing the railing.

He barrels down the stairs, sometimes jumping over some of them, sometimes almost falling flat on his face, his whimpered curses and terrified gasps echoing until he disappears down the street.

How am I related to that piece of shit?

I turn back to Karin. "Hey, are you all right?"

She looks at me, her eyes red from crying, and shakes her head.

"Okay. What can I do for you?" I ask very carefully.

She throws herself into my arms.

3

KARIN

I couldn't stay in my apartment after Terry's attack. Not even if I got drunk. After I got a comforting hug and my tears under control, I asked James to take me to his hotel room.

ON THE DRIVE OVER, I wasn't thinking about sex. I had a pain in my arm, the strung-out feeling of an adrenaline hangover, and the memory of Terry ambushing me on the other side of the door when I took out the trash. I hugged myself as I sat with James in the back of an Uber, driven by a friendly older man.

Now, however, as the glowing, golden tower of the hotel actually comes within view, I start to relax as the reality of the situation sinks in. Terry is gone—forcibly ejected from my life. He was the most repulsive dick before James made him stop. I'm finally free of him.

. . .

My thighs draw together, thinking about what will happen next. After all, I told James I wanted to breakup with Terry before I spent the night with him. Right now, I am not sure I'm quite ready.

"Did he hurt you?" James asks softly as our driver pulls into the parking lot.

"Just some bruises. He didn't hit me, but he grabbed my arm hard and pushed me back into the door." It's the most physical that a boyfriend has ever gotten with me—even the guy who broke into my apartment.

Of course, I mistook that poor bastard, Alan, another sad sack with a violent side, for a prowler; it took me half of a minute to grab a bat and clout him upside the head.

When I realized he was my ex, abusing his copy of my key, I hit that fucker again. I'm not proud of that, but it kept him from hurting me. I just wish a weapon had been handy when Terry grabbed me.

"I'm sorry. I should have stayed with you. I'm glad I thought to double back." He seems genuinely troubled as our driver pulls up in front of the hotel.

"It's fine. I'm glad you came back." I stare out the window at the thin snow falling, then grab my overnight bag as the sedan halts to a stop.

. . .

THE CHILLY AIR bites at the back of my neck and knees as I step out. James offers his arm; my hand hurts a bit as I grab it. "I'll key you in a tip. Thanks again," he tells the driver, who smiles and drives off.

AS WE APPROACH the lobby doors, I stand close to James to shield myself from the wind. Another winter is descending on New York. I'm so damn tired of all this cold. I wish I could go back to the West Coast ... but I can't go back home.

DON'T THINK about that now. Terry's given you enough miserable shit to deal with without going over years' old family drama. I take a deep breath and walk through the hotel doors with James instead.

"If you want, I'll have a look at your injuries when we get upstairs. You don't appear well right now." He is so authentic, it puts a lump in my throat.

I CAN'T REMEMBER the last time that a guy showed concern for me. Early on, Terry had his sweet moments, fumbling and cute, like a wilted flower handed to me by a small boy. Once he thought he didn't have to work for it anymore, even those scraps of affection dried up.

AND THE TWO GUYS BEFORE, or my family? I let out a soft, sad snicker as we approached the elevators. "No. I'm not okay. And thank you. I'll need to take photos in case I press charges."

. . .

"I've got you covered. I even know a good local lawyer if you need one. I seriously doubt he'll be back after this, though." I don't drop his arm in the elevator. It feels like a railing I'm grabbing in a high wind, keeping me steady.

Under the thick wool coat, he's as firm as carved wood, intriguing me enough that it distracts me a little. And his spicy cologne, which smells so exotic ... I wonder what country it's from. "I don't want to resort to a lawyer. But ... I'll definitely file for a restraining order."

He's quiet as the elevator rises toward the penthouse. "This isn't your first time dealing with someone with a ... bad temper, is it?"

A part of me wants to bitterly laugh and tell him the truth: I've been dealing with bad-tempered, abusive scumbags since I was born. "No. I just had some bad luck."

"Undeserved, for certain. You're a wonderful person. My aunt was hoping for a marriage as you're better company than just myself at her holiday table." He shoots me an apologetic smile.

"Never happen." The disgust in my tone makes him laugh. It's incredibly liberating to talk to someone besides Samantha about Terry.

. . .

THE ELEVATOR STOPS and a drunk-looking couple piles in, immediately leaning into the corner to kiss. The girl's sparkly black dress rides up her hip as he strokes it, and she moans invitingly into his mouth.

FIVE FLOORS LATER, they're gone again, leaving me flushed and dry-mouthed, my eyes a bit wide.

JAMES' smile is wicked now. "They definitely have the right idea," he comments, and I stifle a nervous giggle.

FINALLY, we reach the penthouse, and he leads me to its broad, white-columned expanse. We remove our snow-crusted shoes at the door and my aching feet sink into soft gray wool carpet. I sigh with relief and stop for a moment to get my bearings.

HE COMES up behind me to take my coat and I gratefully shrug out of it. The air inside is warm without being stuffy, and scented with a wisp of incense. "First, you need to relax," he murmurs in my ear. I catch my breath, feeling my nipples tighten under my blouse.

Apparently, Terry has ruined our relationship, but not my sex drive.

AFTER YEARS of being stuck with men whose behavior killed my desire, it is incredible to feel the yearning so strongly. It's James' doing. In the year between our two meetings, no other man has affected me like this.

. . .

ONLY JAMES.

"YOU'RE RIGHT," I sigh, and let him lead me to a broad leather settee, long enough to stretch out on. I sit on the edge and watch him shuck his coat, the pewter-colored suit jacket, his tie—and then, to my surprise, his shirt.

I'M STILL in my velvet dress, watching a man I barely know, but desperately want, strip in front of me. He casts his fancy clothes aside, as if they're a disguise he wants free of as soon as possible. "Ugh," he mutters in passing. "What sadist invented ties?"

MY EYES WIDEN as he stretches up to remove the clinging silk undershirt beneath, watching the muscles ripple across his chest and belly. The tiniest hints of dark auburn hair peek out of his belt-line just below his navel; my eyes lock on them hungrily for a moment. He strips off the wad of fabric and tosses it with the rest.

"HOPE YOU DON'T MIND. I'm done with suits for the evening." His eyes flicker and then he heads for the wet bar. "Would you like a hot toddy and a massage?"

WATCHING him walk away in his suit pants is pure torture. His tight, broad-shouldered back ripples with muscle, and a pair of deep crimson wings is tattooed across it, highlighting his shoulder blades and the elegant sweep of his lower back. My eyes trace down to his ass beneath the wool and wonder how far down the tattoos go.

Oh God. I'm struggling for breath. Now that is dirty pool. "I—I don't mind," I manage.

He's seducing me, slowly, gently enticing me with his body, the stylish surroundings, his unaccustomed kindness. It's not what I'm used to.

Nevertheless, these little tastes of his attention, his flirtation, make me want more.

"I hope you don't mind me asking. How did you end up with Terry anyway?" he comments, holding a brown ceramic mug of toddy. I take it and sip it, the honey, whiskey, and lemon mix pleasing to my tongue.

"I get lonely. He was in my movie club. We had some hobbies in common."

It sounds so tame now. I don't tell him the lamest part, though. The part where every single guy I've ever dated has been a huge step up from the last, and even the worst of the three were better than my father—or my brothers.

. . .

"I'M CRITICAL OF YOU. You're just too beautiful and charming to settle for the likes of him." He sits beside me on the chaise longue and takes a sip of his own toddy.

"GLAD YOU THINK SO." I laugh nervously, too aware of how close he is to me. My fingers curl around the cup as I squash the urge to trace his tattoos with them instead.

"LET'S have a look at your arm," he says tenderly as he reaches out and crouches in front of me. I stare at him for a moment, then push the bell sleeve back, revealing the developing reddish marks. He winces, holding it gingerly; the finger marks are clear.

SILENTLY, I begin crying as he takes photos of the injury. It's too much like the past. His camera phone clicks and for a moment I'm twelve years old, in a room of a police station, shivering in my underwear as a camera chronicles the bruises all over me.

THE FLASHBACK GOES AWAY and he's still tapping away at his phone. "I'll send these to your email." In a low voice, I give him the address and he finishes up.

"I'LL CHECK your back next. Do you mind lying on your stomach?" His voice remains gentle as he lays his phone aside.

I NOD and stretch out on the davenport and he straightens up. "Where does it hurt?"

. . .

I POINT OUT THE SPOT, on the left, above the small of my back. In response, he unzips my dress down to my waist.

I SUCK AIR AND FREEZE, but he folds the fabric away and tugs it down on the side with the bruise. "Oh yeah, that's going to leave a mark too. I'm so sorry. Do you want a pain pill?"

"No, I had some before dinner. I was kind of, uh ... anticipating a headache." He chuckles and I chortle with him.
"Your muscles are so tight. You sure you don't need a bit of help loosening up?" And with that, his warm hand settles against my back, and instinctively, I feel like extending under him.

"I DIDN'T KNOW you give massages," I murmur, laying my forehead against the pillar of my arm.

"OH YEAH, this is how I made extra money at resorts in the summer." Both of his hands are on my back, tucking the top of my dress aside, smoothing over my bare shoulders.

MY EYES FLUTTER CLOSED, and my heart starts beating faster. His hands move up and down my back, tenderly caressing at first, having me get used to his touch. The warm, soothing strokes expel my past, banish thoughts of Terry, and leave me shivering with pleasure.

. . .

"Do you like that?" His breath tickles my ear as he whispers into it.

"Yes," I manage, scarcely loud enough to hear.
   "May I bare more of your body, then?"

I feel my whole midsection seize, thighs squeezed together with sudden hunger. I know what he's doing. I know where this is going.

I want it more with every passing second. With growing desperation, I can only pray he's as good at fucking as he is at seduction.

"Yes."

4
KARIN

I hear the rasp of my dress zipper lowering further, and then cool air on my skin. I sit up just enough to slip my arms out of the sleeves, and lie back down. His hands are on my skin again, and I forget everything but that.

I only realize how rigid my muscles are when he starts to knead them, his powerful hands soothingly rubbing me over until I relax enough for him to knead deeply. My back pops several times and I gasp, going almost limp. I'm entirely in his control now.

And I love it.

The most I've ever felt with a guy has been frustrated arousal and a wistful sort of comfort. This is already different. He's only touched my bare back so far, not even unfastening my bra. And I'm already swooning.

Even Samantha seems to think I need to get rid of Terry as soon as humanly possible. I don't even feel guilty about it. Instead, the idea that Terry would scream in helpless rage because I'm spending the night with his cousin fills my heart with defiant glee.

To hell with you, Terry. You had eighteen months with me. This man's already done more with a backrub than you ever did with your prick. As if that's where happiness lies.

And then James' hands move to my sides, down to my hips. Briefly, his fingers dig into the hollows at the tops of my thighs and I whimper, arching my back. "God, you're exquisite," he murmurs, tugging the dress down off my hips to expose my panties.

I feel the velvet slide out from under me and a flush of heat runs from my scalp to my breastbone. It feels like a conclusion is being made—not irrevocable, but definite. There it goes.

His hands settle on the backs of my thighs and knead downward slowly, heading toward my still-aching feet. I moan softly, and bite my lip when he cups one foot in his manly, long-fingered hands and kneads the pain away. Then he switches to the other ... and by the time he's done, I'm so relaxed, it feels like I'm floating.

He straightens up, and then I hear the rustle and zip of his trousers. Then he crouches beside me again. "Did you enjoy that?" he murmurs in that same mesmerizing tone.

I turn my head to face him, panting softly. His eyes burn with desire, but he hasn't yet touched me intimately. Only relaxed me ... while at the same time teasing me with what he can do with those hands of his.

"Yes," I whisper.

He smiles tenderly. "Good. Would you like me to kiss you?"

I offer my mouth at once, eyes closing shut—and feel his warm, ample lips capture mine. His hands start gliding over me again ... and this time, it's purely sexual; I feel it all down to my toes. The kiss lingers, almost lovingly ... and then breaks as he leans back eagerly, gazing down at me.

"Where else would you like me to kiss you?" One of his

fingers slips under the edge of my panties from behind and teases them down a little, and I give a desperate wheeze of pleasure.

"Everywhere," I whisper daringly, my head already fuzzy with desire.

He smiles.

A minute later, I find myself digging my fingers into the frame of the settee, whimpering with every breath as he leaves a trail of kisses all the way up my spine. Each long, rough peck sends jolts of pleasure through me, making my pussy tighten with need. When he finally unhooks my bra to work his way up, I barely notice.

His own breath shivers against my skin as he leaves his marks on me. Meanwhile his hands slide over my body and then slip in front of me to loosen my bra cups to help me remove it. As he does so, his fingertips brush over my breasts, which makes me jolt and utter another whimper.

He keeps leaving his marks, even on the backs of my thighs, while he firmly kneads my ass. "Roll over when you're ready," he mutters. Another rustle of cloth—and then the crinkle of a condom wrapper.

I'm a touch disappointed, expecting him to push to fuck me the moment I roll over. But this is still more foreplay than I've ever gotten. I hang on for as long as I can as he keeps teasing and caressing me, until I can't take it anymore and roll onto my back.

There's a mirrored wall beside the chaise longue, and my pale figure is draped across it, breathing hard, nipples firm and tight. James rises from his crouched position and looms over me. He's naked and hard.

His cock seems as thick as my wrist, and nearly as long as my forearm; it throbs against his belly, the skin so taut it shines. He's rolled the condom on, but instead of climbing onto me, he leans over and kisses my mouth instead.

Eagerly, I return the kiss, reaching up to caress his broad shoulders. He's shivering with desire, the barest tremors running through his muscles as he fights back his zeal. Then he takes both of my hands ... and lays them firmly against the leather.

"Right now is all about you," he declares, looking deep into my eyes. "It's about the woman in that mirror and making her feel good. Don't distract yourself trying to please me. I'm fine."

Surprise rushes through me and I stare at him ... then slowly turn to look at the panting, trembling girl in the mirror. James walks to the end of the divan and gently tugs my panties off my legs and flings them aside. The girl shyly stiffens for a moment, and almost raises her hands to hide her body.

But orders are orders ... and from the right guy, they're hot as hell.

I close my eyes as he caresses his way back up my body, tracing every curve. His mouth suckles and nips its way from my neck down to my breast and covers every bit with soft kisses.

Then he sucks my nipple into his mouth and pulls at it firmly. My eyes fly open. The white sylph on the sofa writhes as my eyes blur; I dig my nails against the leather and sob. Nobody's ever ... not even this much ... it's so good ...

One of his hands settles on my other breast, fingers starting to stroke and tease the nipple in time with his eager lips. The other drifts to my wet, aching pussy and grips it firmly. Then it starts to pulse, sending jolts of pleasure through me.

"Yes," the woman in the mirror cries out. I keep my hands off him, my nails sore from digging my fingertips against the leather.

I squirm, heels sliding down as he works his hand to my pussy. The air burns pleasantly in my lungs as I gasp for air; I've never been so provoked. The scent of his cologne and the musk beneath it mix in my nostrils with the smell of my own arousal.

I briefly feel his teeth graze the edge of my ribcage before he kisses my belly and darts his tongue into the shallow crease running down to my navel. His hand leaves my tingling breasts, the nipples so hard and sensitized that they're a little sore, and slides from my hips to my thighs, parting them softly as he moves to the end of the chaise longue.

I'm not sure what he's up to until he firmly grasps my hips and pulls me to the edge, neatly looping my legs over his shoulders as he crouches down. My butt lifts up; one of his hands slides beneath it to support me. I gasp, startled, shocked, and delighted ... my heart beating hard.

He grins wickedly at me through the fringe of his hair, swept by his passionate movements. His eyes burn at me, promising things I can barely imagine. Next, he starts kissing his way up my inner thigh.

When he breathes over my pussy, stirring the sparse hairs adorning my mound, I whine softly. It takes everything I have not to touch him with my hands. My legs tremble; he props them open, nestling between them while my toes curl in midair. He parts my lower lips with his fingers and leans in for a long, delicate kiss.

It's the only way I can describe it; his tongue slides between my labia with the same delicacy it did with my mouth, teasing me open, stroking every fold and leaving me wide-eyed again. The ceiling swings past my eyes as he lowers his lips further and starts lapping at me slowly.

In school, a friend of mine once complained that she'd never met a New York guy who ate pussy. Apparently, this man, like his family, formerly from the Bronx, is a blessed exception. As his tongue strokes and circles my clit, I lose control of my voice and mewl and sob, begging for more.

My head rolls against the leather upholstery, nails still digging into it, feeling my cunt tighten some more with every lash of his tongue. My hips lift, rocking against his face; I don't care how I look. I only want this amazing sensation not to end.

He slides his finger into my cunt as my muscles tighten around him; I gasp, and then groan encouragement. He slides another finger inside and starts stroking me from within, stirring me up even further. "That's good," I gasp aloud, "So good, oh baby, don't stop ..."

He doesn't. He's merciless, his free arm pinning my legs to his shoulders as he speeds the lash of his tongue. My voice breaks into cries; I feel my belly and thighs and hips constrict more and more as I start to shudder uncontrollably.

Suddenly, I'm rocketing toward the unknown, my whole body thrumming with ecstasy, anticipation, and alarm. I let out a high, strangled gasp—and then I scream, blaring with pleasure so intense I can barely stand it. It feels like I'm airborne from inside.

He holds me firmly, never breaking the rhythm of his caresses as I thrash and wail my way through my very first orgasm. He feasts on me, even after the sensation has lightened. There's a delicious sense of satisfaction rolling through me. No; he won't allow it.

Instead, before my body settles, his swirling tongue pushes me back up the mountain again. It frightens me; and leaves me somewhat out of control. I've given all of myself to him—and he's not ready to let go.

Three fingers are in me now, stroking me from within as he licks and suckles. I don't know if I'm begging for him to stop or go on; I have no idea how I can hang onto the couch instead of his muscled shoulders. Then I entirely lose my bearings in another flood of pure ecstasy.

I phase out for a few moments; when I wake, he's climbing

onto the chaise longue and pulling me up onto his lap. I can see his stiff cock between my thighs; then he seizes hold of it and tucks the bulky top into me. He thrusts upward as he pulls me onto him ... and sinks into me with a long groan.

I brace myself, sensing his caresses from within as he thrusts deeper and deeper. Lastly, he's buried inside of me, and as he shudders and his chest heaves, for a moment, we remain still.

Then he starts moving.

It's amazing how much time he takes tenderly easing that enormous tool in and out of me as his body flexes and quivers against mine. His warmth is sinking into my bones. I roll my hips a little, to tease him, as if I'm using the last of my strength.

"Lie back," he instructs in a husky voice, his eyes hooded. I do, and he tosses his head, letting out a small shout as my cunt tightens around him. I don't understand the angle we've assumed until he starts to move again—and I gasp in shock as the head of his cock rubs firmly against the same spot his fingers tickled before.

I wrap my legs around his hips as he lays the heel of his hand against my pussy and presses down as he thrusts. "Oh, that's good!" I gasp, as he chuckles softly and speeds up.

Words fly away; the leather slides under our naked bodies as our voices degenerate to primal grunts. The slap of skin on skin grows louder and faster as he drives more and more desperate cries out of me. I feel another explosion gathering ... this one even more intense than the first.

He's too far gone to stop now, his whole body and mind engaged in fucking me, his voice just as loud as mine as he loses control of himself. His back arches, and the roar of ecstasy sets me off. We grind together, trembling, drawing from our pleasure together until we collapse into a limp, balmy tangle.

"Oh," he rumbles, expression blissful as he holds me. "Oh. Fucking you is heaven. Let's take a nap in and do it again."

I've never felt so relaxed or satisfied in my life ... or such affectionate gratitude. I can't speak yet, so I smile sleepily and nod instead. Then I drift off, before he can even withdraw from me.

5

JAMES

I wake up in the hotel room with a gorgeous naked lady curled in my arms and my cell phone buzzing in my coat pocket across the room. Reluctantly, I walk, naked, to grab the phone, into the bathroom, shutting the door before answering. "Yeah?"

"How'd the meeting go?" Andrew's terse rasp permeates in my ear and I roll my eyes.

Fuck. Now I have to think.

"Christ, Andrew, don't you sleep?" I sigh. "It's fine. I got Herschel to cough up another ten percent." Trust Andrew to kill my afterglow with business talk.

"And the delivery?" His tone doesn't relax. Of course it doesn't. Not about this.

I keep calm and reassuring. "The courier's been on the way as of two hours ago. Your share will be there by five a.m. I guess you'll be awake."

"Until I have my share of that ten million, yeah, I'm not sleeping a wink." That's Andrew: insomniac, borderline paranoid, distrustful as hell—even of us. He can be a giant pain in the ass, but he's exactly what we need when researching building schematics or hacking a security company or bank computers.

I'm our entry man—I can defeat physical or electronic security systems, climb walls, and break into—or escape from—almost anywhere. Dale, meanwhile, handles lookout and getaway. However, without Andrew, there are no schematics, no guard change schedules, no research.

It pays to keep the paranoid bastard happy.

"Suit yourself. Anyway, it's done. I'll be back in New Orleans on Monday evening. We can have a meet early Tuesday." I know exactly what I'll be doing for the intervening three days.

"You're staying over for the weekend?" He sounds suspicious.

"I have family here. I'm visiting them for Thanksgiving. It's my prerogative for being in town this week." Actually, I could give less than two shits if I see the three of them again before Christmas. Karin is, undeniably, another story.

I would visit New York City again for Karin any damn time.

"Oh. Right. Forgot." His tone goes back to coldly neutral. "We have to talk about the next job when you get back. Our target in Chicago just got some mob security."

"Shit. Might not be worthwhile at all." The last thing we need is to piss off the Chicago mob. Their guys have fenced our jewels, stamps, coins, and other goodies more than once.

They have dirt on us, and a lot more power than we have. That's not an enemy we should make.

"I agree," he replies solemnly, sounding slightly relieved that we're on the same page. "We'll go with something else."

Caution and discretion have kept the three of us out of jail for over ten years. That is why I always give at least half an ear to Andrew's paranoia. The aging, growly-voiced hacker has avoided run-ins with the law for longer than I've been alive and his caution has been warranted eighty percent of the time.

"We're not exactly short on prospects. Anything else going

on over there?" I already miss New Orleans. The steamy heat will feel good after New York's bitter cold.

"Dale's dealer got picked up and he's whining about it." Now he sounds exasperated. I snort and shake my head.

"That's definitely not the end of the world. There's a dealer on every damn corner during the holidays; we'll find a new one." I heave a sigh. "Hold the fort over there, Drew. I gotta get some sleep."

"See you Monday then. If the package doesn't show within two hours, you'll hear from me again." He hangs up before I acknowledge.

I sigh with relief and pause to look at myself in the mirror. He'd bitch at me nonstop if he knew I'm staying longer because of a woman. I wipe a trace of Karin's lipstick off the corner of my mouth, before killing the light and going back to bed.

When I get there, Karin is restless. She whimpers slightly and tosses. There is tension on her face. Nightmare?

A tear leaks from beneath her closed lids.

Yup. I touch her shoulder, shaking her gently. "Karin?"

Her eyes fly open and she sucks air, hyperventilating with high, desperate sounds, like screams in reverse. I grab hold of her at once and pull her into my arms; she clings to me, trembling and burying her face in my shoulder.

"Oh God," she sobs. I sit on the bed and gather her, and the bedsheet around her, into a bundle on my lap.

I hold her and stroke her hair, speaking softly. "It's okay. It is. It was just a dream, sweetheart."

She shakes her head and clings to me more tightly. "It was a memory," she finally mutters.

Oh. Well, shit.

"If it's that fucker Terry—" I start, but she shakes her head more slowly.

"Just hold me," she asks delicately. "There's nothing ... else to be done."

I do. That part's easy. With a fierce, knife-keen anger that startles me, I still want to know who hurt her.

Hold on there, hotshot. You barely know the lady. Don't get attached too quickly.

It's tough, though, with her warmth and fragrance in my arms, clinging to me like this. "Okay. I don't know what's going on exactly, but you're out of harm's way with me."

She slowly relaxes, and replies, "Thank you."

"No problem." I nuzzle the top of her head and then set my chin on it. "I've had my share of nightmare memories. I know how it gets."

That seems to calm her, and she shifts her grip from a desperate cling to a warm embrace. As I look at her hair, I smile and close my eyes.

"That's better," I mutter. "You need to talk about it?"

She hesitates. "I don't want to unload on you this way."

"I asked." I'm not in much of a mood for a big therapy session with a new lover, but I doubt that's what this is about.

I can tell when someone has toughed their way through a lot of torment. There's a kind of survivor's pride that kicks in, along with a desperate need not to be a broken burden. They don't ramble about their problems forever.

After a pause of silence, she says in a gentle but matter-of-fact voice, "My dad liked to beat the crap out of us. My mom, Samantha, and me, I mean. He never touched my brothers. They were boys, so he liked them.

"My mother did nothing about what he did to us. She was probably glad somebody was around to take her place as a punching bag. She was more interested in pleasing him than protecting her kids." She sighs.

"They don't sound like suitable parents," I comment, and she nods. "Good you got away from them."

"I got a scholarship at a school on the East Coast just to do so." Her voice shakes slightly. I pet her back for a while and she unruffles.

"That's how you learn where to file for a protection order. You've already done it." Damn it. This poor woman. I'd like to beat her father's face in.

My fury on her behalf startles me again. I don't know how anyone could not care when faced with a story like this but … this is more. It's already starting to feel personal.

"Yeah." She leans back and smiles up at me thinly. "The first ones I ever filed were against my father and brothers. My sister did the same. She just didn't move so far away."

"But they've never actually come here to New York, have they?" I ask tentatively.

She shudders. "Once. After my dad got out of jail, he tried to visit my dorm. I wouldn't open the door. He punched the security guy who removed him and ended up in jail again."

Again. So Dad was a criminal. Wonder what her take on criminals is.

"That sounds harrowing." I catch her eye as she uncurls slightly. "Do you have anything for self-defense?" I can't help but think of Terry, whom I still feel like kicking off this planet.

"Just a lot of pent-up rage. Weapon laws in New York City are crazy." She sounds annoyed. I wonder how long she tried to find a single proper self-defense weapon.

Maybe I should give her some self-defense lessons. I can't always be here to protect her. But at least she can learn some basic principles. Like not giving a fuck what is legal, proper, or nice.

I smile and nuzzle her cheek until she raises her mouth for a delicate kiss. "Laws are crazy, period. Sometimes you have to ignore them to survive."

"That sounds like a good way to be arrested." Her brows draw together as she peers at me.

I run my thumb over her lips. "If it comes down to survival, fuck the law, and fuck being nice and decent. You have to protect yourself first."

She frowns ... but then nods slowly. "I'm just a bit scared of what I might do if someone actually tries to hurt me. After everything, I might go bonkers."

"Then do it, sweetheart. If your life is on the line, do whatever it takes." I grab her chin and look into her eyes. "I want you to promise you won't restrain yourself if Terry, or your family, or anyone else comes at you."

She blinks in surprise, and I feel the warmth of her skin under my fingers. "Even if it means to really hurt them?"

"If they're going to hurt you, they deserve it, plain and simple." I lean down and kiss her again. "Do what you have to."

She nods. Her eyes widen and dilate as she gazes up at me. *You have a need for some direction, don't you? From someone who cares, someone you can trust.*

And suddenly I'm hard as a rock all over again, and aching for her.

"I promise," she says, and I smile back at her.

"Good." I settle her back on the bed, unwrapping the sheeting from her like the paper on a present. The bruise on her wrist has developed further; no restraints on her for at least a few days. But this time, I want her hands on me.

She stretches out on the bed, her nipples tight and her eyes going soft and bright with desire. Looks like the nightmare's lost its grip on her; I take hold of her instead.

After what she's been through, she needs gentleness. Slowly, tenderly, I caress her, kissing her neck, her breasts, rubbing her skin. I avoid touching the marks Terry left on her, and with my fingertips tease the ones I can, until she trembles.

Entering her soft, warm body, feeling her arms and legs hold me closer while she whispers encouragement in my ear, I feel too much tenderness; it's risky. Except the warning voice goes away as she stretches under me and moans, and I sink deep into her to feel her contractions.

She's so much fun to make love to, especially now that I realize how much she's been missing. She clings to me, writhing under and around me, gasping for more.

I go slow, relaxed, drawing it out, even as the tension in my loins threatens to go off like a bomb. I slow down, panting for air, as her body shudders with pleasure, trying to hold out as her orgasm threatens to touch off mine.

Then her hips grind reflexively—and I blast off, feeling like I'm emptying my balls into her all at once, the gratification so extreme that I hear myself shouting hoarsely and can't understand what I'm saying.

For a long time, all I can do is quiver in her arms.

Then I settle over her, sighing with such deep contentment I can't even think of moving to get rid of the rubber yet. That was too fucking good. I want more of this. Maybe every night.

That worries me faintly but I feel too good to pay much attention. As I close my eyes to rest them for a few moments, another thought interrupts my bliss: the realization that I was shouting her name.

... shit. Oh well, no helping it now ...

When I open my eyes again dawn is breaking outside. Disoriented, I look around: oh, the hotel room. Karin is nestled against my naked torso.

The delectable sense of relaxation, of fulfillment, slows my thoughts as I lean over to nuzzle my sweet little bedmate's tousled curls. I like her, I think, with a growing sense of warmth. I really like this one.

It's only happened a few times, especially since I got into the business. It's easier to keep women at arm's length when you have to lie about where you've been, what you've been doing, and of course, how you earn money. Now and again, though, a lover will get too close, and I'll hurt both of us by breaking things off.

Melody, a jeweler who re-cuts and sets some of our stolen gems and re-casts the gold from their settings, is the only lover I've had who is actually in the business. We broke it off in a friendly way when she got serious with some guy with a vanilla job. That's the closest I've ever gotten to falling in love.

Right now, though, looking at Karin's sleeping face, I'm already feeling more than that. It's worrisome. Too soon.

And how in the hell can I maintain a relationship with a smart woman like her without telling her what I do for a living?

I sleepily move away from her—and then feel it. My eyes fly open as I become fully awake in a split second.

Fuck, the damn condom. I fell asleep inside of her, wearing it.

I retrieve it, peeling the mess off my cock as I walk to the bathroom. Did it spill? If so, did it spill inside of her?

The worry passes after a moment. Probably not. What would be the chance anyhow? It's probably fine.

I'll just tell her about it tomorrow.

6

KARIN

"So, I'm leaving on Monday, but you're welcome to stick around as much as you like until then," James says as he brings me breakfast in bed. It's crème brûlée on French toast with strawberries, a mimosa, and some tea, delivered by the room service. He lays it on a tray across my lap. I sit up against the pillows, the bedsheet draped across my chest.

"I would really like that." I'm completely dazzled by this man and what he's done, and I can't wait for more.

Of course, I promised Samantha to have lunch with her before she goes back to San Francisco. Great sex and great company tempt me to stay, but she's the only family member who is loyal to me. That's vital, no matter how huge of a crush I have on James.

"The other thing I want to propose ... and this is a bit early, but I wanted to give you time to think about it ... if you want a break from this fucked-up winter, I have a loft in New Orleans.

You could stay for a week or so." His eyes search my face so hopefully that I realize this crush isn't one-sided.

Say what? There's so much more about this man, it floors me. How can this wealthy, hot, amazing lover be smitten with someone like me?

I smile way too wide, my cheeks warming. "It is a little early. But I like the idea. And I really like you. I'll ... I'll think about it."

His eyes light up. "Good."

When I pick Samantha up for a late lunch and a movie, she notices right away that something's up. "Hey, did that hot guy James actually stay over after you dumped Terry?"

"No, James didn't stay over. There was an ... incident after you left." She gives me a stern look. I pulled over for a minute to explain and nod.

She pales slightly. "That son of a bitch put his hands on you? I wish James had tossed him over the railing!"

"Terry's gone. James took pictures of the bruise on my arm. I already filed a protection order this morning."

. . .

"Good. I should have punched him in the teeth. How's the Black Friday traffic?"

I smirk. This is New York City. The first time I merged into traffic on my way from the airport, I almost had a panic attack.

"Everyone in New York state drives like they have to pee or are an inch from murdering someone, so ... typical." Los Angeles had equally nasty traffic snarls when I was learning to drive; Angelenos aren't quite so aggressive.

She chuckles a little nervously. "I trust you can handle it then."

I do, although we see three fender-benders in the snarled traffic before reaching the theater.

The movie is some forgettable bit of science fiction going on in front of me as I sit in the dark, thinking about James. I squeeze my thighs together, tingling all over, recalling what an orgasm feels like.

The taste of his mouth. The smell of his skin. The way it felt when his whole body went absolutely taut, shaking helplessly, his face transformed by ecstasy.

. . .

I WANT MORE. The images of laser-space battles and improbable aliens blur into the background as I dwell on the image of James and I in the mirror as his cock pounded into me, both of us wild with desire, legs clasping him tight as I grind my hips.

I'M DEFINITELY GOING BACK to his hotel tonight. My pussy is already aching for him as I sit next to my sister.

"WELL, that was ... a waste of thirty bucks. Let's get some food," Samantha chuckles as we walk in the thin snowfall afterward.

I NOD, starving. Breakfast in bed went right through me. I guess good sex burns a lot of calories.

WE GET BOWLS OF RAMEN, hers with shrimp, mine with beef, and elaborate mochas piled with whipped cream and candy shavings. We take seats at the crammed bar; every table is full of exhausted shoppers and their whining, tired kids.

"SO, once you got rid of Terry, what happened between you and his hot cousin?" She leans toward me conspiratorially, a gleam in her eye.

I wink at her, wondering how much to tell. But my cheeks are already burning, and a grin spreads across her face as she sees it.

. . .

"I spent the night with him. I couldn't go home anyway." As if that somehow excuses spending hours fucking a man I've only spoken to twice.

"So? How was he? You seem way relaxed after the fiasco with Terry, so … pretty good?" Her eyebrows bounce. "Level with me, already!"

I press my lips together, cheeks heating even more. Finally, I giggle. "He was amazing."

"Goddamn, girl, at last! I was wondering if I had to set you up with one of my friends. So, will you see him again?" She takes a bite of her ramen as she waits for my answer.

"Yes, definitely." There is no damn way I'll let him go.

"He lives in New Orleans, though, doesn't he? You guys ready for a long-distance romance?"

I take a few bites of ramen to buy myself time. James invited me to go with him, at least for a while. I'm rather uncertain.

"He's talking about us spending a week down there." My cheeks are still burning.

. . .

Samantha stares at me speculatively for a few seconds, and then slaps her hand on the table. "I say go for it."

I blink at her in surprise. "Sis, wait ... that's kind of hasty. Why?"

"Because the guy makes you smile. Because New York is fucking miserable in late November and you hate it here. Now that you're done with school and Terry's gone, nothing is keeping you here.

"Go check out New Orleans for a week with a hot guy. See how you like there—it's got to be better than this place. I swear to God, at this point, you could take your business to any state and do just as well."

She reaches over and pats my hand. "I know you've worked hard to make a place here. And I know you won't go back to Los Angeles. But staying here can't be easy since you've been attacked on your own doorstep."

I nod, swallowing a lump in my throat. "I bet if there wasn't snow everywhere, you'd be happier visiting me for holidays."

"Oh, you know it," she chuckles. "So anyway, what does James do for a living? Last night he mentioned he's in security, but never shared details."

. . .

"He's doing business with two partners. They create custom-built security systems for mansions, jewelry stores, things like that." James was vague about it over breakfast, mostly more interested in me, and how I was feeling.

"Must be pretty good to afford the fancy suits. Did he actually rent a penthouse suite?" Her eyes twinkle with mischief.

"Um ... yeah." Probably a good thing; my screams of elation would have disturbed any guests sharing our floor.

Even he hollered that second time. His panting, passion-filled cries are in my mind as I slurp the noodles—and rub my thighs under my skirt again. Karin ... Karin! Oh yeah, baby—ah! Karin!

"Damn. Your first proper fuck and it's a rich, hot business owner in a goddamn hotel penthouse. Not bad, sis." She snickers as I blush again. "Not bad."

"I guess so."

"I know so, honey, you're glowing. You're going back for more later?" Her eyes glimmer. "Knowing you won't be alone tonight after this Terry thing would be great."

. . .

I SHAKE MY HEAD, thinking again of his body against mine. "Oh, I definitely won't be alone tonight," I utter with a lopsided smile.

7

KARIN

I take my sister to the airport and drive back to town after our lunch, the crazy traffic hardly bothering me. My head is full of last night and New Orleans and James.

I go back to my apartment to get some fresh clothes before going to the hotel. My place looks tinier now, and though the inside is still a charming little haven, I shudder when I cross the doorstep. The room is still haunted by Terry.

I briefly go around throwing everything of his in the trash: mostly cheap beer, empties, and printouts of his favorite fad images. I never let him leave much stuff and now I'm extra thankful for it.

Once that is over, I grab a few outfits and toiletries and put them into my smallest suitcase. I don't want to come back often in the next few days.

My old-school, cheap answering machine is full of messages. I ignore the flashing light as I walk past; I already know who the hell they all are from and I don't want to hear from him. I can use the recordings later as evidence against him; he's not supposed to be calling me.

You had your chance, Terry. I look around for anything else

to bring with me. The emergency protection order has barely taken effect and you've already violated it. Good job, you idiot.

While I'm packing up, the phone rings again. I ignore it.

I grab the pies and make a few sandwiches, bag them up, and put them in my reusable shopping bag. I don't have the funds for room service, and I don't want to assume that James will just keep paying. Besides, depending on how long he's in town. I'm not sure if I'll have much time at home to eat all these leftovers.

New Orleans. He really asked me to go to New Orleans with him.

The suitcase is a little heavy, but it protects my stuff. I pull the bar up to roll it behind me and sling the handles of the shopping bag under my arm, with the pies balanced precariously on the palm of my hand. As I open the door and pull out my keys to step outside—Terry is right there waiting for me!

He lunges at me from a few feet away, face twisted and purple with rage—and the adrenaline hits me like a billion icy needles stabbing inside of my veins. And that's when I don't see Terry anymore.

I see my father instead.

I shriek, and the pies fly into his face. He stumbles back, grunting and flailing at the mess obscuring his vision. A metallic clatter barely registers in my ears.

The keys are between my fingers and I punch him in the face. He stumbles back a few more feet. I strike him again, and now there's blood mixing with the chunks of apple and smashed pumpkin drooling down his scraggly chin. He tries again, and I beat at his throat. He barely tucks his chin down in time and gets a slash there as well.

My hand hurts; it's bleeding. I drop the keys and unsling my shopping bag. He bellows like an angry bull and rushes me again, too crazy with rage to realize his face is mangled. I grab the suitcase and hit him right in the face. He yelps in shock. I hit him again; his arms fly up to shield himself and I drive the handle into his gut instead.

The whole time, I'm yelling at him, the same word over and over, not even coherent, like a battle cry, punctuated by the blows. "Fuck you! Fuck you! Fuck you!"

And scary, abusive Terry stumbles back from me, teary and snotty as a kid after a fall. "Ow! Owww! Ow! Karin, stop, you're hurting me—ow! Stop! I wasn't going to do anything! I was just mad about the restraining order! Stop! STOP!"

I hit him in the face with the suitcase again, flattening his nose in a crunch and spray of blood. "I told you not to come back! I told you to leave me alone!"

"Yes. Yes, you did, but how could I—"

"I said leave me alone!" I hit him again, and he stumbles, teetering at the top of the concrete staircase leading to the street. "Get the fuck away from me!" *You crazy, dense fucking imbecile, what does it take?*

"You don't mean that—" he starts, and actually reaches out to me and takes a few steps forward. "You love me. You're mine."

"No!" I slam the corner of the suitcase into his balls.

His eyes widen and his knees buckle; he folds over at the very top of the stairs, and then overbalances. He tumbles halfway down the stairs and then wads up against the railing, knees up, cradling his groin. "You ... you heartless bitch!"

"I hate you. And I belong to myself. You have ten seconds before I call the cops about the restraining order violation. Make them count." I pull out my phone.

For a guy crying about my hurting him, he sure gets up fast to run for his battered Dodge when I mention the police. He's too out of shape to even cross the parking lot before I call the cops and give them the information—and his license plate number.

Goodbye, Terry.

Only then do I look down at my hand, which is torn up between the fingers from using the keys. Oh well, it worked.

I turn to walk back to my open door—and that's when I see it, gleaming on the concrete walkway right next to my welcome mat.

A goddamned eighteen-inch Bowie knife.

My knees collapse under me. I stare at Terry's knife, realizing that the blitz attack I was just starting to feel a little guilty about literally saved my life. With shaking hands, I grab my phone to call the police again and share this terrifying new information.

Then I call James.

"You doing okay?" he asks the moment he hears my voice.

"No. I'm gonna be stuck at my place for an hour or so." My voice is shaky. "I'll come back to the hotel after that." He shouldn't deal with a bunch of nosy police because his cousin tried his hand at resentful killing.

I look back at the knife. The knife I can't carry for self-defense because Terry could show up at my door in response to the ineffective protection order. The cold seeps into my skin, and I shake my head.

Fuck New York.

"I think I actually would like to visit New Orleans with you." I really already wanted to—but now, it feels like a need.

"I'm curious why you came to your decision so quickly," he replies. "Come back when you can, all right?"

I smile, already feeling a little better. "I will."

The police find Terry hiding in a parking lot two blocks from my apartment building. He's weaseled his way under one of the cars, so they bring in canines. The call comes through that he's in custody while I'm being questioned.

When I identify him in the line-up, his arm is bandaged and swollen from where the dog fastened onto him. Karma is a bitch.

While I'm giving my report, his mother calls my phone twice. I let it go to messages and don't even listen to them. I know she's begging me not to press charges, just as I know that the stupid, enabling bitch will be paying his bail.

Neither one is my problem anymore.

By the time it's over, I'm so exhausted that I hire a car to the hotel. That fucker Terry slashed all four tires while I was inside, packing. When the driver drops me off at the door, the snow is really starting to blow.

I swear, I am only staying in this fucked-up city long enough to testify. Then, whether it's to New Orleans, San Francisco with Sam, or somewhere else, I am moving the hell away.

"Shit, I should have gone back with you," James' eyes widen as I walk in, spattered in pie, and one hand wrapped in gauze. "What the hell happened? Are you okay?"

I answer with a nervous laugh as I step into the room, dragging in the two plastic bags the police gave me. My suitcase has been entered into evidence. "Um ...Terry made a mistake."

I'm wrung out from adrenaline, but it's different this time. I won. I'm not the one bleeding. Not much, anyway.

He locks the door behind and takes my bags, then leads me over to the couch beside the chaise longue and sits me down. "Okay. Tell me everything, including if I need to kill him."

For a moment, I think he's showing off: playing the tough guy to impress me. Then I see the rigid look in his eyes and realize he is genuinely irate. I stiffen, swallowing nervously, and his face immediately softens.

"I'm sorry. I don't mean to upset you more."

"It's okay," I breathe, calming down. "I'm not used to guys being angry in my defense instead of at me."

"Yeah, well, I keep hearing about jerks that hurt you. Of course I want to be the guy that helps you get revenge."

I try my best to lighten the mood by flirting with him a little.

"So, spoil me," I tease gently. "Living well is the best revenge of all."

He kisses me ... then looks down at my hand. "Did a medic get a look at this?"

"Yeah, I just tore up my hand using my keys to punch Terry in the face a few times."

James goes quiet for a moment as his eyebrows slowly rise. "Wait, what?"

I explain the whole thing, blow by blow, through my desperate assault using pie, keys, my suitcase, and a lot of yelling. As I reiterate, James' face journey is amazing: first shock and rage, then astonishment, then mild awe and growing delight.

By the time I send his cousin tumbling down the stairs clutching his balls, James is laughing so hard, he has tears in his eyes.

I smile sheepishly. "So yeah, I did exactly what you told me. I didn't hold back."

"No, you didn't. Oh my fucking God, you are amazing. I'm keeping you. C'mere." And he hugs me tight, apple chunks and all.

My heart swells and I smile against his chest. How the hell can I feel so good this soon after the worst breakup ever? It's all him. I want to keep him too.

He orders some tea to warm me up; I've been outside in the chill for hours. I sit and sip it as I fill him in on the rest. "Of course, nobody came outside this time either. I'm starting to think that a lot of New Yorkers are a bit sociopathic."

"You're probably right about that. This isn't a good city for you. It wasn't for me either." He picks an apple chunk out of my hair. "How about we table this until after you get cleaned up?"

"Sounds good to me," I say, pulling off my pie-spattered coat and carrying it gingerly into the bathroom with me.

I deliberately get cleaned up before looking at myself in the mirror. I don't need to get depressed again. I rinse off my coat, clean up after that, and hang it up before undressing and stepping into the shower.

My hand is slightly crusted with blood under the gauze. I won't need stitches, but it's still nasty looking. It stings as I rinse it off.

I did it. I actually fought off that piece of crap and saved my own life. I'm amazed at myself! Amazed at how much having the right man believe in me and instruct me to look after myself helped me find the strength.

James wants me to protect myself. He sees me as worthy of protection, and he doesn't want me saying or doing otherwise. No matter what my father, Terry, and fuckers like them keep saying, I am worth protecting.

"I'm really proud of you, sweetheart. You want some help cleaning your hair?" James asks through the door.

A tingle runs through me and I beam. "Yes, please, come join me!"

I hear the door open and he steps inside. There's the rustle of him shedding his clothes, then the shower door rolls aside and he steps in behind me.

He grabs a sponge and the soap and lathers up. "Get yourself nice and wet under that spray, sweetie. I'll take care of you."

As the sponge glides over my skin and his free hand starts to do the same, I shiver happily and start to relax. Every awful, ugly, humiliating, uncomfortable thing I have gone through since going back to my apartment is slowly draining away, like the chill from being outside. We laugh over the bits of pie in my hair, and he laments that my delicious leftovers became weapons.

Next time I have access to a kitchen, I promise him pie. He says he'll hold me to it.

It feels like James is washing the last vestiges of Terry off of me, bathing me in his touch and scent as much as in soap and water. Everything, even the close call I didn't know was a close call until I saw that knife, fades firmly into the past. Terry's in jail; I've blocked his mom's phone number; and I?

I'm going to New Orleans.

8

KARIN

As soon as the plane levels and the fasten seatbelts sign turns off, James starts stripping. I blink at him in mildly fascinated confusion as he shucks his jacket, sweater, and turtleneck, leaving him in his clinging T-shirt. When he unbuckles his belt, I blink and say, "Uh, babe, there are a couple of nuns across the aisle. Should I cover their eyes?"

"Oh, don't get up on my account, honey!" one of the nuns calls out, sending me into a blushing fit and making the sister next to her snort and poke her on the arm.

James chuckles. "Sorry to disappoint. You'll join the Mile-High Club when I get a pilot's license." He shucks his trousers to reveal a pair of loose blue cotton pants.

Still bundled up, I watch as he packs his shed clothes and tucks his bag back under the seat. Now I know why he brought it half-empty. "Is it really that hot in New Orleans?"

"As we say locally, 'it's not the heat, it's the humidity.' It's like New York right before a thunderstorm—warm and wet. But don't worry." He pulls a package from under the seat in front of him. "I brought you a change of clothes too."

Inside the box is a silk gauze outfit, deep ultramarine to go with his deep blue, a tank dress, and a filmy shawl to camouflage the bruise on my arm and all the hickeys he's left on me. "Wow." I didn't expect gifts, especially this soon.

Heck, Terry never got me a single thin. I could get used to this.

I end up changing in the airport, already sweating even with the air conditioning. I slip into the women's room, shed my New York camouflage, and come out a California girl on vacation. Outside, winter has turned into summer.

"You look lovely," he purrs as I take his arm. "I'm going to show you everything I love about this town."

It starts pouring down—warm, steamy rain two minutes after we leave the airport. James lets out a laugh and turns on the windshield wipers. "Guess the walking tour of the French Quarter will have to wait."

"I don't mind. This is dreamland after that entire fucking chill." The habitual tension of New York City is leaving me, minute by minute, as I gaze out on the damp streets of the Big Easy.

New Orleans in the rain. I roll my window down partway and the steamy scent of the city blows in at me. Rain, river water, car exhaust, half a dozen cuisines, wet greenery, and ozone. I hear a faint rumble of thunder far away; the wind is rising.

I'm glad I came. Right now, I barely care if I go back. I just want to live and be happy for a while, with nothing crazy going on.

"You look happier just getting out of town," he notes.

I look at him and smile, nodding. "Thanks for this. After everything, I can't even tell you how grateful I am to get out of the city for a week." And I can't ask for better company.

"I have a couple of meetings with clients and my partners

this week, including one late in the morning tomorrow." he says optimistically. "Other than that, I'm all yours. All I request is that you not be shy about asking for things. We just finished a new business deal and I'm feeling prosperous."

"Better watch it; you're tempting me to take advantage," I tease, and he laughs.

"I'm not worried about you asking for too much. I just want to make sure you don't ask for too little. I'm in the mood to spoil you." He winks, and as we cut through the thin afternoon traffic, I squeeze my thighs together, along with taking a shivery breath.

Nobody in my entire life has said that and actually meant it. And even though it's probably stupidly premature, I feel myself fall for him slightly more.

His loft turns out to be on the top floor of a converted hotel on the edge of the Garden District. It's mostly one big room, ancient ship-lap on the walls and the floor, and ceiling beams made of equally old and heavy timber. The whitewashed walls neatly contrast with the dark wood; the windows are heavily screened and draped in pale gauze.

A complete home gym dominates half of the main room's space, including a baffling array of poles, ladders, perches, and handholds covering the walls and hanging from the ceiling. It almost looks like an obstacle course—or like James flies around when he's home alone.

The rest of the loft is about what I expected: a high end, unusually neat bachelor pad, complete with a huge entertainment center and a couple of pinball machines in one corner. Other than that, the space, though beautiful, is rather plain.

"This is lovely," I comment, walking over to look at the sixth-floor view. From this high up, the wet street and its inhabitants blur into blobs of saturated color, like an Impressionist painting. "Do you have a lot of guests here?"

"Just my partners, or the occasional friend or lover. Actually, you're the first lady I've had over in a long while." There's a thoughtful note in his voice as he takes my bag and takes it to the master bedroom door. "Would you like the nickel tour?"

"Sure." I ignore the minor discomfort when he mentions having other lovers over. Don't be ridiculous.

I follow him around the main chamber and into the bedroom, which is one of only three rooms with actual doors on them. It's a big, airy space, dimmer than the others, and dominated by a broad bed with a massive oak frame.

To my surprise, the corner of the room has a wrought iron spiral staircase going up. "What's up there?"

He smiles. "That's the rooftop garden. It's mine as well—actually, the whole building is mine. I rent to friends, and the few businesses on the ground floor.

"Upstairs is kind of my sanctum. It's a bit hot to use the Jacuzzi, but later, after the storm, it will be cool enough."

The idea of screwing in a hot tub excites me ... but not in the current heat, and surely not on a rooftop in a thunderstorm. "I'd like to have a look once it cools down."

"For now, I'm going to grab my bong and make a couple of mint juleps. Have you had them before?" He steals a kiss as he breezes past me, showing me the bathroom before walking through the broad kitchen archway.

"Mint juleps? No, never. Are you trying to get me wasted?" I lift an eyebrow.

He pauses and, in the same cheery tone, asserts, "No, I'm trying to get me wasted. Care to join me?"

I stifle a giggle. "Sure."

God knows I need to relax as much as possible after Terry. And I trust James. If he takes advantage of me while I'm high as a kite, I'm sure it will be something I end up ... thoroughly ... enjoying.

"How long have you been in interior decoration?" he asks as

he dumps an enormous bud into his grinder and pops the cap back on. The juleps are already half-empty; it's hard to savor a drink when the ice melts in a few minutes. "I need some help with this place; also with some of the lower floors. They're quite bland."

I look around thoughtfully. "You have almost no art or plants, and your color scheme is blacks, dark browns, and whites. You could use some mid-tones and other colors besides brown."

"You think so? Thing is, I like keeping my walls clear. I guess I could have a mural." He looks around.

"What about stained glass and light catchers? The crystal ones? Those would color your walls with nothing in the way of your ..." I look around at all the stuff on the upper walls. "Obstacle course? What is all of that?"

"You've basically got it. I'm a parkourist and a caver. This is where I practice when I don't have time to do it outside."

I stare at some of the more improbable perches and handholds and then blink at him. "Uh ... do you fly?"

He laughs merrily. "No, I've just had a lot of practice and built up my strength and limberness." Which is also why he has such an amazing body.

"I'll gladly demonstrate if you'd like."

"Later," I say, amused by how eager he seems to impress me. "Bud now, Air James later."

He snorts and starts to load the bong.

Twenty minutes later, I've finished my drink, melted ice and all. My lungs burn from a lot of coughing, but a tingling sensation has eased through my body. I'm lying in the crook of his arm, on his enormous couch, talking about how to decorate his loft.

"You prefer all your plants upstairs and none indoors?" I feel good. My nipples tighten. I haven't had this much good pot since smoking with one of my college professors.

"Yeah, they're all upstairs. I take advantage of the fact that it doesn't drop below freezing here. It changes how things grow." He cuddles me close as we smoke.

Once the bong bowl is ashed and I'm so loose and peaceful I'm almost dozing off, he helps me up to show me the rooftop garden. In my drowsy state, the climb up the spiral staircase takes some effort—but then he opens the rooftop door, and I disregard my temporary discomfort.

We emerge under a large, screened-in gazebo with rain tapping on it; the hulk of a twelve-seat Jacuzzi takes up half of the space underneath. I walk up to one of the screens and glance over a broad swath of green dotted with flowers and fruits. It's like summer in late November.

He loops his arm around my shoulders. "Do you like it?"

I don't know what it is: the booze, the pot, everything that's happened, James himself. But the sight of all the greenery brings tears to my eyes. "It's incredible."

"Hey," he says, instantly concerned. "Hey, what is it?"

"Oh, it's silly." I wipe my eyes impatiently and force a smile. "In New York, I get so depressed over winter. This makes me not want to go back."

There's so much more to it, but I don't feel like ruining the moment with a long whine session. I just know it now: New York has become too uncomfortable for me to stay. Now, thanks to Terry, almost as many awful things have happened to me there as in California.

"Don't think about going back then. I can give you enough work so you can stay here for at least a few months. Would breaking your lease be a problem?" His voice is so kind, my eyes brim over again.

"I'm sure I could get someone to take over my lease in under a week of searching." I take a deep breath. "I just ... guess we shouldn't get ahead of ourselves."

"No. And you shouldn't worry about going home when you've barely gotten here." He kisses my chin, then the end of my nose, teasing me before kissing my mouth. "Forget about seven days from now. Forget about yesterday. C'mere."

And he pulls me into his arms.

I am falling for him more and more as he holds me close, and I keep reminding myself I barely know him. We might not get along long term. Problems may crop up.

But the future is undefined. At this moment, his warm caresses make the sadness go away, and banish my overthinking. I wrap my arms around his neck and he lifts me, delicately twisting with every step as he carries me downstairs.

The pot makes helping each other out of our clothes into a comical, fumbling exercise, with a lot of kisses and wandering hands. He lets me explore his body this time, quivering in delight as I trace my fingers over his back and lightly run my nails lightly over his ass. But when I start trailing my hands curiously toward his groin, he chuckles and nudges my hand away. "No petting, dear. I want it to last."

I settle for helping roll the condom onto his magnificent cock, which I want to stroke and kiss but simply sheathe, eager to feel him inside me again. Then he's nudging me back against the pillows, settling over me as I wrap my arms and legs around him.

I moan as he fills me, and feel his body shudder as he pants for control. Then he leans up on his arms and kisses me tenderly, moving his hips slowly as my body shivers and tingles under his touch. "Karin," he whispers reverently, and the heat in his voice makes my toes curl by itself.

We slowly move together, his lips and fingers teasing my body, which is already sensitized from the pot. When his hand dips between us to tease my clit, I feel myself edge up to an orgasm fast. In response, he slows his caresses deliberately, keeping me in that blissful frenzy that comes just before.

Almost mindless with lust and pleasure, I writhe under James, crooning with bliss, my eyes squeezed shut. He holds me, fingers stroking my receptive flesh as he slowly thrusts. And gradually, tease by tease, he leaves me clinging to him, trembling ... begging.

"Oh please," I gasp breathlessly. "Please ... don't stop ..."

"Not yet," he rumbles maddeningly, his hand and body never speeding up against me. When I rock my hips, he slows further. "Not yet."

I lie back, completely high on sensation and shuddering with frustration at the same time. *No, please, finish me off ... I need it ...*

He holds out and holds out, moving slowly, even as both of us tremble and pant with restrained passion. Frustration slowly gives way to submission. He stares into my eyes, and I feel myself swoon under his gaze, a strange, deep peace filling me as my inner muscles tighten with a desperate need for release.

"Do whatever you want with me," I hear myself whisper, and mean it with all my heart.

He smiles. "Good girl."

Ultimately, he speeds up, moving with solid thrusts, growing faster and rougher as he loses control of himself. I cry with joy and lift my hips to meet his, and we roll around on the bed, tangled together as he pounds away at me tirelessly, our grunts and cries in unison.

My back arches as the satisfaction gathered in my clit finally explodes in long bursts, leaving me sobbing with ecstasy. James quivers and lets out one of those little pleasure shouts that tells me he's close, and I grind against him wildly until he thrusts deep inside me and his shouts rise into a long, husky groan.

I collapse, exhausted by the long-teased, explosive climax; when I open my eyes again, James is climbing back into bed with me. He snuggles against me from behind, wrapping an arm around me.

Filled with serenity and protection, I quickly drift off.

9

JAMES

Later that night, a strong thunderstorm rolls in; the sound of hail shattering against the reinforced windows awakens my appetite. I open my eyes onto my darkened bedroom and turn briefly to look. Karin's here, curled up next to me, head on the pillow beside mine, like she belongs here.

Maybe she does, I think, and the rush of warmth troubles me again.

But I'm getting less worried, I realize, slipping out of bed to take a shower. I'm starting to like the idea. Except for one tiny, nagging thing.

"How do you earn this much running a security company?"

I have to tell her the truth, I think as I soap off our sweat and her perfume. The faint nail marks she left on my biceps sting a bit, making me smile in spite of the serious subject. I should spoil her first, get her used to the money, before I disclose where it comes from.

Either way, I scarcely know her, and I'm already tempted to take the risk.

By the time I get out of the shower, I'm starving. I need a

steak; my training diet isn't nutritious enough to maintain all this fucking. And there's no way I'm quitting anytime soon.

I dress in a clean pair of shorts and a black T-shirt and saunter into the main room, making a beeline for the kitchen. I'm walking past the couch when Andrew's voice speaks up from it.

"So, who's the girl?"

His voice is neutral but curious. The fact that he's here, in my home, without being invited, tells me two things. He already suspected I'd shacked up with someone, and either he doesn't like it, or something's so fucking urgent, it demands a face to face.

Also that I should beef up my security again, using even less-hackable electronics.

"Jesus, Andrew, what the fuck are you doing here?" I complain as my shock dies down. Instead of addressing him directly, I walk past him to the kitchen, pull out a couple of marinated steaks and a can of beer, and start fixing myself and Karin a proper meal.

"You've been lying to me," he replies in the same cold tone. "You had other reasons for staying in New York, and now you've got a girl with a suitcase in your loft and we have a meeting tomorrow morning. It's not like you."

He appears at the end of the counter, squinting, as I turn on the lights over it. He's a compact, lean man with a narrow fox face, sunken pale blue eyes, and orange hair he crops close.

"Is that woman why you stayed in New York for three days when you can't stand it there?"

I start searing the steaks, doing the edges first so the fat melts into the pan. "Okay, first off, you're way the fuck over the boundary here. And not just because I find you camped out on my couch while I'm entertaining a lover. How fucking long have you been here?"

"Half an hour."

Well, at least he wasn't listening in. "You go through my computer?" I snap, looking over at my desk.

He glances that way and shrugs one skinny shoulder. "Of course."

"Asshole." I leave the steaks to sear on one side as I crack my beer open. I'm too annoyed to offer him one. "I didn't lie to you. There was a debacle with my family and I needed the weekend. She's involved."

"How big of a debacle?" His eyes narrow. "Something to worry about?"

"No. It's strictly a New York-my family kinda chaos. My cousin got himself arrested because he went full Norman Bates on the lady. I was the only one willing to deal with the situation. So I did."

His eyebrow rises. "Seduction is how you deal with Terry's abused girlfriend?"

I snort. "That happened separately, more or less. But yeah, she's here for a week. She wanted to get out of New York to unwind after dealing with it."

"And now you have a house guest that you're fucking, and hiding it from us." His scowl almost looks like a pout.

"Nobody's hiding anything. We got into town four hours ago. I was going to tell you at the meeting."

He grunts acknowledgment, uncertain if he believes me or not.

"Anyway. Tell me how who I screw is any of your business?" I flip the steaks and take another big swallow of my beer.

"It becomes my business if your pillow-talk lets anything slip," he snaps back. The muscles in his lean jaw work.

I eye him for a moment. "Drew. The girl knows nothing; no situation with her involves you; and it's not like it'll get in the way of business if I have an active sex life."

He scowls and glances away. "Yeah it is. Women want attention. They want to know why you come in at three in the morning. And they don't just notice every goddamn thing—they fucking gossip."

"You sound like a manosphere blogger. Knock it off." I can understand why Andrew doesn't trust women; his wife tried to roll over on him as fallout from their divorce. But that doesn't give him the right to stick his big damn nose in my stuff.

"Fine." He pulls out a cigarette and puts it between his lips.

"Go out on the balcony to smoke, it stinks," I grumble, finally handing him a beer.

"It's raining out." But he doesn't light it. He takes the beer and glances at the bedroom door. "I know you don't plan to give us problems."

It's not quite a question. I sigh hard and preheat the oven. "If I was planning to betray you, the money wouldn't have been in your hands before I left New York. I would have grabbed the whole ten million and taken the fuck off."

Sometimes I get so tired of Andrew's paranoia and total lack of any manners that I want to punch him. It may keep us safe sometimes, but it is incredibly hard to live with. It's one of the reasons the three of us never got a big place together; I would never have been able to have friends or a lover over.

He grunts and tucks the cig behind his ear, taking a drink. "You have a point."

"We've been working together for ten fucking years, Drew. When are you going to trust me?" I'm already getting a headache.

Lightning flashes and I see his bitter smirk outlined in the hard light for a moment before he goes back to scowling. "I don't even trust myself, James. That's how I stay out of jail."

"The girl's not a problem," I say decisively.

"Give me her name, then. I'll do a background check."

I burst into low, incredulous laughter. "Oh for fuck's sake, Drew, really?"

He stares at me implacably.

"Fine," I mutter. "But next time, give me a phone call when you have questions for me. Don't break into my place."

He snorts and drains his beer, his Adam's apple working in his narrow throat. "Just helping you find the holes in your security." He crushes the empty can and sets it on the counter. "See you at ten."

"Walk out the door like a normal person," I tell him, but he's already out on the balcony, where I can see a grappling hook on the iron railing.

"We're not normal people, James. Don't forget that." And with that, he's gone.

I sigh and shut the door. Of all the hackers I could have ended up partners with, I had to get the one with a Batman complex and no sense of boundaries. On the other hand ... I'm confident he won't find anything troubling on Karin, no matter how deep he digs.

So, fine. He'll make inquiries, reassure himself, and it'll be over. I pop the steaks in the oven on high heat and stroll to the fridge again for the makings of a salad. He'll shut the hell up like he does every time his paranoia is off beam.

Lightning flashes, and the thunder rumbles almost on top of it. Outside, the wind moans in the eaves of the old building. Crazy old bastard, climbing cables up the wall in this downpour.

Dale has an innocent streak and sometimes needs things explained to him in small words, but he's dead stable. Andrew ... he's fucking brilliant, but I take turns being annoyed with him and worried about him. And he needs to stay out of my house when he's not invited.

I check my watch. It's not even late: ten o'clock. I consider my phone for a few moments. Aunt Caroline has called six goddamn times since yesterday. I know she'll beg for bail money.

I frown. Part of me wants to call her and explain why I'm not going to help this time. Part of me wants to see her grasp the truth about her son: that he's gone from being a whiny disappointment in life to a genuinely dangerous failure at life.

It's great Karin beat the shit out of him. It's somehow more satisfying than doing it myself.

I finish chopping the tomatoes, cucumber, and avocado into the lettuce and squeeze lemon juice and olive oil over it. Then I sprinkle on some herbs and garlic and have a taste. Perfect!

I check the steaks and slice up some sourdough to go with our feast. I'm sure Karin will wake up hungry, and I want to astonish her. She's not the only one who cooks.

Setting the table, I think about Andrew's warning, and how tempted I am to tell Karin everything. I don't want to lie or hide things from her; that will end up being a deal-breaker if it comes up later.

And it will. If a relationship lasts long enough, these things always come up. I haven't really done love, but the same damn thing happens with good friendships. I know better than to consider long-term deceit with a lover.

Especially Karin, who has been betrayed and disappointed by every man in her life. I don't want to be another link in that incredibly fucked-up chain. I'd rather be the one who breaks the cycle, for good.

But unless she knows what I am and what I do, there is nothing permanent between us. If I reveal myself as a professional thief, and she can't accept it, the exact kind of problem Drew warned me about will occur. And I would do what he fears: expose us to someone who goes to the police for help.

Damn. What do I do?

I look back at the simple meal and smile slowly. I reach into the middle of the kitchen floor and open a trapdoor, which reveals a spiral staircase leading to the wine cellar. I've been collecting bottles since I made my first million a decade ago.

She always goes for the red wine at dinner. I descend in search of a bottle twice my age.

The plan I came up with runs through my head as I retrieve a 1958 Barolo and uncork it to breathe. The scent of wine mixes with the scent of herbs and roasting meat, and I grab a slice of bread and cheese to tame my growling stomach.

Once the meat is resting and the candles are lit, I walk back into the bedroom to wake my lover.

Spoil her, I think. Spoil her until the idea of being with a crook doesn't sound so bad. Then tell her.

10

KARIN

"So how was New Orleans?" Samantha's voice on my phone fills with mischievous excitement.

I LAUGH AWKWARDLY. "Uh ... well, I'm actually still there, um, here."

IT'S BEEN ten days since the plane touched down in New Orleans, and the thought of taking off for New York City and my tiny apartment has barely entered my thoughts. James has been busy dazzling me, and I've been active ... getting attached.

I'VE SEEN every museum and historical site, drunk generations-old wine, and toured the Bayou in a fan boat. I've tasted absinthe and gone on haunted house tours. I'm dressed in silk; I have diamond studs in my ears.

If James isn't trying to keep me, he's doing a damn good job of faking it.

"What? What about your court case against Terry? What about your apartment?" She sounds almost horrified, as if I've lost my mind.

I ignore the heat creeping across my cheeks. "I sublet it to a friend, Sam, it's fine. I couldn't stay in town anyway after Terry made bail."

"But you're going back to testify, right? That piece of shit needs to be in a cage." She's been on a vendetta since learning I was being attacked by Terry while she was flying cross country.

"Yes, I absolutely am, but with the backlog he probably won't get a hearing for four months."

"Four months? And meanwhile he gets to walk around free? What the hell?" Her voice cracks a little with outrage; she's been fighting a cold.

"Yeah, now you see my problem. Or part of it. The case may be moved up if he keeps violating, though." Which he does, constantly.

. . .

Phone calls and emails from multiple numbers and accounts to get past my blocks. A drift of threatening letters forwarded from my sublet, Carl, and sent on to the NYPD.

Carl's a professional bouncer and ex-Marine. The first time Terry showed up on the doorstep with another knife, Carl exploded out of the door, took the knife away, pitched him over the railing, and called the police. The second time, he just leaned out with a camera and took pictures while Terry ran.

Those were sent to the cops as well. Apart from taking him back to jail for a while, they're of little use. It's frustrating … but since I'm out of town, it's not really my problem.

"Okay, okay, I can understand why you don't want to go back right now. At least tell me you have some positive reasons for staying in New Orleans." She sounds worried.

I scramble to reassure her. "Of course there are. And not only James, although he's still as amazing. I have a couple of projects I'll be doing over the next few months."

"Not more small stuff like daycares, right?" Her skepticism sets my teeth on edge, but I shake it off.

"James' loft and an art gallery owned by a friend of his." Big bucks and big references. Exactly what I need to get my business to the next level ... and grow some local roots.

I'VE FALLEN in love with New Orleans, just as I'm falling for James. The sights, the people, the food ... the lack of snow. They have some impressive storms rolling through in this season, but all I get in them is wet.

Mosquitoes are many. and vicious, especially by the water ... but they're not much worse than the ones in New York during the summer.

"THAT ... actually sounds like you're doing well down there. What will you do when you have to testify?"

"COME BACK FOR A FEW MONTHS, wrap it up. Then, if things continue to go well over here, my lease ends in April. Once Terry is convicted, there's nothing tying me there." And good riddance.

"AND JAMES? How's he treating you?" Her tone goes cautious. She's heard me gush about him twice so far, but after everything that's happened, she's protective.

"HE'S SPOILING the heck out of me, Sam. I have never experienced anything like it." I lie back on James' couch, stretching out luxuriantly.

. . .

Some of it, I can't even tell her about. Like how we've been experimenting with silk scarves and blindfolds, now that my wrist has healed.

Like the slightly sore spots on my ass where he smacked me last night until my cheeks were tender and my cunt ached for him.

Or, alternatively, like my uncertainties about James' line of work.

"Well, good. You deserve it. Best to start working down there, though. Don't depend on a guy you don't know very well." There is warning in her tone, and I understand it; after Terry, I'm cautious as well.

"Don't worry, I have enough to put myself in a hotel or even on a plane if James unexpectedly gets weird on me." Which might still happen; it's been nearly two solid weeks of fabulousness, but we're in that honeymoon period at the start of a relationship.

Something may still go wide of the mark.
However, it's curious how he get all this wealth from a small security company. Why his hours are so odd. And why he deals with everything in cash.

. . .

THE MYSTERY only grows as the weeks continue. He's never short on money, never worried about bills, never talks about deadlines. His family's poor, so he isn't sitting on an inheritance.

WHERE DOES IT COME FROM? Why doesn't he talk about his work? And why have I met friends of his from all over the city, but not his partners?

IT ALL COMES to a head New Year's Day, when I wake up sick to my stomach.

"I DON'T KNOW what the hell is going on," I ramble as James helps me up from kneeling in front of the toilet. Breakfast was, apparently, a mistake. I ate eggs and toast without so much as a gurgle from my stomach, but one bite of the sausage patty made me run for the bathroom.

"IT'S DEFINITELY NOT A HANGOVER; you only had a goblet of champagne." He hands me a glass of water. I rinse my mouth, spit and flush, turning to brush my teeth. "Maybe a doctor should examine you."

"YEAH, THIS IS KIND OF TROUBLING." It's only been one day but if it's something contagious, I want to know.

I END UP GOING TO JAMES' doc, an old German lady who practices in her converted domicile. She has tough gray eyes, iron-colored curls, and is blunt, but kind. Regrettably, one of her first questions alarms me.

"How long has it been since your last period?"

... Oh shit. "Maybe two months. Although it's intermittent when I'm stressed, and my ex kinda ... tried to kill me."

"Well, that could cause sufficient stress to delay ovulation, however ... I'm going to run a few tests." Her knowing look worries me even more.

Half an hour later, she knows what's "wrong," and so do I. In her words—my body's working as it's supposed to, and my symptoms are what to expect early in a pregnancy.

I'm astonished as, walking out to the small waiting room. James stands up and rushes to my side. "Hey ... you okay? You're white as a sheet."

I look at him and moisten my lips, then swallow and take a deep breath. The words won't come out. "Um, it's not life-threatening ..."

. . .

But, without a doubt, life-changing, and I'm not sure what to do. Except to deal with it—and that means James needs to face it as well.

"I'll tell you when we get home."

He nods, looking dubious and concerned. Same looks the entire awkward, silent drive home.

When we get to the loft, he sits me down on the couch and makes ginger tea. "Okay," he settles in next to me. "Spill. You have me worried."

"I'm ... between eight and ten weeks pregnant," I announce quietly, bracing myself for turmoil. Shock, denial, maybe even ejection. Nothing James has ever done makes me think this way; I'm just used to men disappointing me.

His jaw drops and his eyes widen. My heart is beating too fast, and nausea creeps up my throat. Oh God, please, I don't know what to do; please don't add this on top of everything.

I want to have a kid. I've always figured I would have a few; I'm not baby-crazy like some, but it was definitely always part of the plan. What about James?

    This is where our twisted romance ends.

· · ·

"Holy shit, one of the rubbers must have failed. What ... what do you want to do?"

"I'm trying to figure that out," I say breathlessly. "I'm frightened. Are you mad at me?"

He stares in amazement for a moment, then gathers me onto his lap and holds me tight. "No, sweetheart. You're used to taking the blame for every damn thing and this isn't your blunder. We have to work things out."

My relief is so enormous, I burst into tears. "Oh God, I thought you'd send me away," I sob as he hugs me.

"No. Nothing like that. I just ... look, this is complicated. You don't know a lot of stuff about me, and a child means commitment. I ... I've got some reflecting to do. That doesn't mean I'll toss you out of my life."

Through my tears, I smile at him, grasping the thread of hope he's throwing me with both hands. I hesitate. "James ... you know I'm crazy about you. Would you ever actually want to settle down with me and have a kid?"

It's a direct query and I desperately need an honest answer.

"Want to?" He sighs into my hair. "Baby, of course I want to keep you in my life. The only dilemma with this pregnancy is timing."

INDEED, the timing is awful. We've just started out. Also, I'm not positive at this point in my life that I'm great mommy material.

IN FACT, the first thing I felt when I learned of my pregnancy was a particular dread: I'll screw this up. I will be a horrific mother, because my parents were terrible.

AND EVEN IF I'm crazy about him—do I want to be tied to someone I know so little? My bad luck with men could boomerang. Except, this time, I'll be stuck.

I COULD VISIT A CLINIC ... but there is no medical necessity. And ... it's James' baby. I want to keep everything of his ...

"I'M ANXIOUS. But you make me feel better. You ... you always do, babe." I nestle against him, trying to calm down.

HE KISSES the top of my head. "I'm stunned but ... look, we'll work it out, I guarantee."

I WISH to believe him but am too busy musing about his full confession: the secrets he's been keeping from me—they may be deal-breakers.

. . .

I LOVE YOU, James, but who are you, really, and what kind of husband or father would you be?

11

JAMES

Karin is pregnant with my child.

The moment I hear it, the fact rips me in half, and each half is instantly at the other's throat. Part of me is shocked, elated, hopeful this means my Karin will stay with me for good. The other half is thinking how to tell her what my business is.

Andrew will shit brickworks if he finds out, so he better not. How can you hide things from a meddlesome, paranoid, genius hacker?

I have to find a way. Because the more I think about this, the more I want it. I want her; I want the baby, our life together, and the whole nine yards.

But can she handle being part of my world? For that matter, can Andrew handle her being part of it?

I better come up with something brilliant. I can't lose her.

She takes a nap in the afternoon and I go to visit the converted warehouse functioning as our headquarters and staging area. Now that things have cooled off a bit, it's time to plan another job. The entire drive down, I'm thinking of Karin, upset about how she might react when she learns my story.

Baby. She's having our baby. I'm going to be a dad. But if she can't handle the truth, everything will go away—including her.

When I walk in, Andrew is already there; he looks up from the bank of computers tucked into the near corner and nods as I walk past him to grab a beer from the fridge. "Dale's running late. Stuck in traffic." His smirk discloses how likely he thinks that narrative is.

"He's ex-NASCAR," I grumble as I slump down at the big craft table that doubles as our meeting table. "Hangover?"

He snorts. "That's my guess. So ... you haven't sent that girl home yet."

The shift in topic catches me off guard. "Her name's Karin, Drew. And no, she's decorating my loft."

"Excuses." His eyes narrow slightly. "Getting emotionally involved is dangerous, James."

I eye him. Considering his feelings about women, if it were his choice, he'd probably push for an abortion and dump Karin. "Not everyone lives like a monk, Andrew."

"So hire a fucking hooker. They know how to be discreet." He avoids looking at me as he says it.

I clench my fist against my thigh under the table and take a swallow of the beer instead of replying. Right now I want to kick his ass so badly, I can taste it. How dare he suggest I can swap Karin with a fucking prostitute?

Deep breaths, dude, I remind myself. In my calmest voice, I say, "Drew, I'll say this once, and I don't want to hear more about it. Paranoia is helpful in many things. But if you don't stop riding my ass about Karin—"

"Fuck. You're in love with her," he snaps accusingly, lips twisted with disgust. "You fell for a girl from the vanilla world. Are you nuts?"

"That's a fucking riot coming from you, Drew. Are you jealous?"

For a moment, he actually looks surprised. "No. Cautious." He looks away. "We can't afford to bring a Yoko into this state of affairs."

First he decides she's as replaceable as a hooker, and now she's Yoko Ono and we're the Beatles. My temples start to throb; I force myself to stop gnashing my teeth, and it lessens.

"She's not a Yoko. She's a fine woman, and not the type to mess up our partnership. I'm handling it. Your reaction is more concerning to me."

He snorts dismissively. "You're not being rational. Pussy makes men crazy."

Ugh, I am going to punch him. "I'm not the irrational one here. You haven't met her, and you're already presuming she'll turn us in."

"I have my reasons. And you're not bothered enough about this." He gets up and walks over, crouching on the chair across the table from me.

"You really think you can hide our industry from this girl? We can't afford a commitment, you know that." His eyes pierce mine and I feel my nails grind into my palm.

"No, you're clearly suspicious and don't trust women, and I'm sick of being around when you're like this." I scowl at him. "Once again, I'm balancing both parts of my life very well. And still, my sex life is none of your damn business.

"Keep your nose out of it. My work and private life cannot separate if my fucking partner won't leave my love life alone," I say in my firmest voice. "I will handle Karin."

The corners of his near-lipless mouth pull down further. "Not good enough."

I slam my fist on the table and he jumps slightly. "Nothing ever is good enough for you, Drew. You keep this up, you'll be looking for a new entry man."

His eyes widen. "You wouldn't."

"I've got ten times the cash I'll ever need my whole life already. You know what the safest, most guaranteed way to avoid jail is? Not fucking stealing anymore.

"In other words—an early retirement," I smirk. "Bet you've never considered that as an option, have you?"

Dale enters, shuffling, out of the rain, trailing a cloud of pot smoke. "Hey, James; hey, Drew. What the fuck are you guys fighting about?" He's a tall, lean Creole guy with skin, hair, and eyes the same rough shade of golden brown, and the youngest of us.

"He's still shacked up with that fucking girl I told you about," Andrew snaps.

"The one who ratted her father and boyfriend to the cops?" Dale gives me a startled look as he grabs a cola from the fridge.

I blink, some of my annoyance ebbing. "Wait, what?"

"I finished my research on your Karin," Andrew growls matter-of-factly. "She turned her dad into the cops at age twelve and again when she was eighteen. She also went directly to the police the instant her boyfriend turned violent."

For a moment, it worries me. When there's a problem, people who call the police as their first option are hazardous to our health—and our freedom. Andrew's dead right.

But he doesn't know the complete account.

"So, while you decided these details make her a ticking time bomb, did you fucking notice what those men did that made her call the cops?" Seriously, my fist, your face. Anytime, buddy.

"Wait, what did they do?" Dale asks, his eyebrows rising as he comes to sit a few chairs away from me. Kid's gullible, but he's got heart and valor by the ton.

Andrew explodes. "It doesn't fucking matter what they did! The point is she uses the police when there's trouble!"

I stand up. "It does fucking matter. Her dad beat the stuffing out of her on a regular basis and then stalked her dormitory.

Terry—you know, my cousin, the douchebag? He went after her with a goddamned knife!"

I look at Andrew, whose mouth is working as he glares at me. "Why wasn't that part of your research? Why don't you look at how far she's been pushed before she has to go to the cops?"

"She's fucking dangerous, James!" Andrew's face turns as red as his hair.

"You're fucking dangerous, Drew. You're using 'security' as an excuse to control our lives and isolate us. Remember when you talked Dale into dumping his girlfriend because she was getting 'too close to the truth'?"

He subsides, blinking and glancing at Dale, whose face has fallen. "What about it?"

"You made him miserable because you didn't like him connecting with women. Now you're trying the same shit on me. You want all of us to be paranoid recluses whose only contact with women is hookers—just like you!"

"I don't have to take this shit from you!" he shouts, and tries to shadow me. I stare down at him coldly, and he hesitates.

"You're the one spewing shit. Drew, I'm extremely sober." I fold my arms. "You can either leave me and Karin alone, or I'll break your face and walk away with my share."

He glares at me, his eyes blank, so deep in his unreasonable hostility that he can't even see he's the one fucking things up. Suddenly, I'm so sick of it that I'll put his ass in the hospital if I don't walk away.

So I do. I turn around, leaving the beer behind, and walk out to the rain. My fists are still clenched at my sides, and when I hear someone running up behind me, I turn at once, ready to fight.

"Whoa!" Dale holds his hands up and I lower my fist. "Dude, are you really leaving? Like, for good?"

I step under the awning and run a hand back through my wet

hair. "Dale ... I know you like it better when we get along, but I won't stand and listen to Andrew lose his shit because I have a girlfriend.

"He should fucking know by now that I'm not going to risk everything we've built just because there's a woman in my life. He expects us to live with his damn issues, but this time, I can't. It wasn't right for him to make you break up with Sherry, and it's not right for him to rant like this about Karin."

Dale leans against the wall and stares at the rain, thoughtfully pressing his lips together. "What if Karin calls the cops, though? You can't trust her not to because she loves you."

"I am not concerned about her rolling over on us because it would mean rolling over on me. And even if she knows, generally, that I'm a burglar, what specifics would she know to leak to the cops? It's not like I'll give her names, dates, and heists, even if I tell her anything."

My head hurts so badly, my eyes are watering. "There's a limit, Dale. If Andrew wants to be miserable, be isolated, trust nobody, and hate women—those are his choices. But he has no business trying to push that shit on us."

"Shit," he mutters, running his hand over his scalp. "This is real goddamn thorny."

"No, man, Andrew's just making it convoluted. It's actually simple.

Having girlfriends won't fuck up our partnership. Drew's suspicion, however, will do that by itself if he doesn't rein it in."

He blinks slowly, his confusion plain. "You think so? He's trying to protect us."

"No, man. He's trying to look after himself while taking advantage of our skills. If he gave a shit about protecting us, he wouldn't be pushing us to take new jobs." I don't know if any of this is getting through to Dale.

"But the girl—I mean, uh, Karin, that's her name, right?" He shifts from foot to foot. Dale's the opposite of a dick, but it's clear what Andrew said is getting to him.

"Yeah." I watch him carefully. Andrew has talked to him about Karin, and he's naive as a puppy.

"If she turned her own father in, why not us?"

I look at him sharply. "The only one of us who acts like he wants to hurt her is Andrew. If he goes off the rails and attacks her, all bets are off. Otherwise, no."

"... Shit. How do we calm Andrew down?" He pulls a joint from behind his ear and lights it, drawing on it nervously.

I don't know—a dart gun full of lithium? That's not fair. Andrew is sick ... he's also being a raging asshole, and letting his illness call the shots.

"Most of the time, he's okay. But anytime something goes wrong, a factor he can't predict or control—like another person—he gets like this." I accept the joint and take a hit, if only to calm down before going back to Karin.

I hold the smoke as long as I can, then blow it out to the rain. "There has to be a perimeter, or it's time for us to go our separate ways."

"I don't want that," he says quietly. "I'll try and talk to the man.""Don't let him mess with your head!" I sigh, shoving my hands into my pockets. "Just because he doesn't want a normal life outside the business doesn't mean we can't. That's some bullshit he determined."

He nods, but the vague look in his eyes concerns me. "You don't think I should have stopped dating Sherry?"

"I think I fucked up by not standing up for you more, Dale, and I'm fucking sorry. I didn't get it then. Now I do." I walk to my car. "Just ... I know Andrew can't trust me to fix anything with Karin. I hope you trust me more."

"Yeah," he mumbles. "I just worry. Anyway, come back later,

after you guys have cooled off. We still need to plan the next job."

What next job? I think bitterly. "Yeah, I will. There's something I need to take care of first."

I am coming clean with Karin about everything, and I'll live with the consequences. She's never seen my partners; she doesn't know who they are. I can't expect her to trust me and bear my child—not to mention, prove Andrew wrong—if she doesn't know the truth.

12

KARIN

James is tense about something the moment he walks in the door. I get up from the couch to help him out of his jacket, ignoring my uncomfortable stomach. "Hey, your hair's all wet. Didn't you have an umbrella?"

He kisses me gently but distractedly. "I wanted to feel the rain."

"That means you're down about something." I pat my hands up and down his damp shirt and look at him worriedly. "What's going on?"

He smiles thinly and hugs me, kissing the top of my head. Every tense gesture makes it seem forced. "I have to come clean about some stuff. It won't be an easy conversation, and I'm sorry."

I feel my heart pounding out of control, so much that I feel dizzy. He sees my face and grabs my shoulders with his hands.

"Wait, sweetheart, don't get upset. It's not about you or the relationship."

WE WALK to the couch and take a seat, his arms still around me. "I should have told you this sooner. Before we got so involved. I wanted to show you ... I mean ..."

I HAVE NEVER SEEN James seem so hesitant. "What is it?"

"I FIGURED it would be easier to hear what I'm going to tell you once we knew each other, and you realized I'm not a bad person—and I treat you well." Something about the uncertainty in his chocolate-colored eyes makes him look younger ... even vulnerable.

IT'S ENDEARING ... but I'm still tense.

"BUT NOW I'M pregnant and everything's rushed?" I try to understand. The way he's struggling; whatever secret he's keeping from me, it's pretty damn big. It's alarming to me, despite his reassurances.

HE LETS OUT A SIGH. "Uh, well ... look. What if I told you that the security company thing is just a side job and not how I make all this money?"

. . .

I swallow hard. Shit. I've had my suspicions about his erratic work schedule and enormous amount of free time.

"It would explain some things," I say carefully.

"Well ..." I watch his eyes track around the inside of the loft, the half-dome rainforest mural on one wall, the dim splashes of color from the strips of stained glass that surround each window. "I'm a cat burglar," he says at last.

I sit blinking at him. For a few moments, I think he's kidding. Then my brain starts connecting the dots.

He's a parkourist security specialist who works a few hours a week but has piles of money and comes from a poor background. A man who won't introduce his "business partners"— because he doesn't want to expose me to crooks. The more he values someone, the more he falters telling the truth about himself.

The love of my life and the father of my child is a thief. Apparently, a very successful one.

"Um," I force out, aware he's watching me nervously. "How often does this ... happen?"

"A few times a year." He seems relieved I'm asking for minutiae instead of freaking out. "It's better not to give you too many particulars."

"No, of course not."

He swallows. "Okay. So, you haven't run away screaming. That's good, right?"

"I ... just ...give me a minute." I rub my temple to soothe a stabbing pain, and then look at him. "Do you plan to keep doing it?"

My emotions conflict; love, fret, distrust, anger that he didn't tell me sooner, irritation at myself for getting attached—and pregnant—before I knew.

"I don't know," he admits after a few moments. "I've given serious thought to quitting while I'm ahead. Especially now. Getting caught would affect you and the baby too."

I chew my lip, my hands protectively holding my belly. "I love you," I say quietly, and feel him stiffen.

"... But?" he queries after a pause.

"I know you wouldn't hurt me. But ... you need connections with other—with other criminals. Are they ... harmless to be around me? Around our baby?" I grip his arm, my tone pleading.

Please just reassure me, because this is too fantastical.

"I won't expose you to that, or them." For some reason, his expression turns grim—almost angry. "I don't want to drag you into that.

"That's how I make my money, and you deserve to know. So there it is." He shyly glances away.

Can I handle this?

I reach out and lay my hand on his chest, feeling his heart beat fast under my palm. "James," I start—but I'm cut short by another voice, one so raspy, strange, and full of rage, it sends a chill through my body.

"You fucking told her."

We both turn our heads and James jumps, fists balled at his sides. A strange man walks out of the shadowed, open door of the bedroom, dripping on the hardwood floor. I catch a glimpse of a dark jacket, wet sprigs of red hair, and rigid gray eyes—then the gun in his hand gets all of my attention. I freeze.

. . .

"Goddamn it, Drew, you crazy fucker—you broke into my house and spied on me again?" James takes a big step toward the guy—and he shifts the pistol's aim to the middle of James' chest.

"Watch it, you fucking Judas. Give me a reason not to shoot you right now." His eyes have a lack of control I like even less than the gun.

"James," I cry, my tone dripping terror. "You said I won't deal with this shit!"

"Shut up, bitch!" the man snarls, aiming the gun at me. "If you hadn't wormed your way into my partner's life, we wouldn't have this problem! I should just shoot you and be done with it!"

"You spill one drop of her blood and I will strangle you with your own intestines!" James takes another step forward and the skinny man points the gun back at him.

"I told you not to trust the stupid slut, didn't I?" he starts, as I look quickly around. If I go through the kitchen, I can put a wall between this creep and me and make it most of the way to the door.

"Don't you fucking call her that!" James roars.

. . .

I BOLT.

I'M UNARMED AND SICK; I have a baby in my belly; and James' partner has turned out to be an obsessed creep with a gun. Suddenly his life of crime has gone from dubious to a total deal-breaker. I have to protect myself.

I HEAR A GRUNT AND AN IMPACT, and then the clatter of something heavy and metallic. "My gun!" the guy yells, outraged.

"Run, Karin!" comes James' desperate cry—and I dive through the kitchenette while the two of them struggle, run for the door, and yank it open.

THERE'S another man with a gun on the other side: a young, light-skinned man with an almost apologetic look. He points the gun at me. "I'm sorry—" he starts.

JAMES SAID to do anything to protect myself, no matter how guilty I feel about it.

I DUCK ASIDE and slam my body into his arms, knocking the gun against the wall and making him drop it. "Fuck you, you monster!" I yell, and as hard as I can, bring my knee up into his balls.

HE GOES ASHEN and falls over, coughing and clutching himself. I bolt down the hall, tears of panic blurring my vision.

. . .

I keep running, headed for the stairs, knowing I'll get a bullet if I wait for the elevator. Adrenaline burns my veins. I can't do this. His partners are appalling. They pulled guns on me!

I clatter down the stairs, hearing muffled shouts behind me. I don't know if James is winning or if they are. I don't know if they'll run after me.

I don't even know if I ever see James again. I'm sobbing uncontrollably as I reach the ground floor. I run through the lobby, ignoring the receptionist calling after me, and blindly race to the streets of New Orleans. All I have is my purse; I'm drenched in seconds.

Still weeping, petrified, I keep running, not certain where I'm going.

13

JAMES

"You let her get away! Now she'll go to the police!" Andrew is yelling, spraying spittle as he scrambles after his gun.

I kick it out of his reach and, with all my strength, kick him in the teeth.

His head snaps back, a startled look in his eyes as strings of blood and shattered teeth fly from his lips. He slams against the wall, bounces off, and lands on his face, hitting his head with a satisfying thud. Then he stops moving.

"What the fuck, James!?" Dale is balled up in the doorway, holding his groin, his face wet with sweat as he pants for air. His pistol is on the ground several feet past him. "Did you fucking kill him?"

"Not yet." I pick up Andrew's gun, check it, walk over, and point it at Dale's head. He cringes. "Tell me why the fuck you decided to help him bump off my girlfriend."

"It wasn't supposed to happen like that!" he protests. "He wanted to make sure she didn't go to the cops!"

I stare at him for three fast heartbeats—and then punch him in the face. "You stupid motherfucker!" I bellow as he winces and grabs his wounded nose. "He came to shoot her, and maybe me. He had you guarding the door so we couldn't get away!"

"No, wait. He wouldn't do that ..." Dale trails off, then his eyes widen.

"Yeah, he would. And he talked you into helping. You bought it because you're a dumbass stoner kid who gets talked into bad shit!" I grab him by the collar and pull him upright.

"Wait, James, please, cool off—" he begs, watching the gun in my hand with terror.

"She's carrying my baby, you dumb son of a bitch! I was going to ask her to fucking marry me!" I can't remember being this angry in my entire life. "You two have fucked everything up! She may never trust me again!"

I'm gripping his collar tighter and tighter; he swallows against my knuckles and gags. "James ... please ... I really didn't know ..."

"Please what? Please don't kill you for scaring her away? Please don't kill you for assisting that mistrustful asshole instead of helping me? Explain what fucking thing you're begging my mercy over, you gullible little shit!" I give him a shake.

"Please ... I'm sorry ... give me a chance to make it up to you!" He stares at me, scared stiff.

The muzzle of the gun in my hand wavers slightly, then drops. "How can you possibly make this right?"

He looks past me, fear on his face. Then his eyes focus on something behind me. "I can help you catch up to your girl before Andrew does," he pipes up.

"What?" I turn—and the spot where Andrew was on the floor is empty save for a swirl of blood and spittle on the floor. "Fuck!"

"There's only one car, and I have the keys," he struggles to reassure me. "If you let me try, I can search the whole area a lot faster than him—or you walking."

I gaze at him—sweaty, pleading-eyed, and still anxious. I nod and lower the gun. "Let's get moving."

It's pouring rain outside. I shove into the passenger seat of Dale's modified Caddy and grab my phone, calling Karin. She has the phone in her purse.

"Come on," I say as the phone rings and rings. "Come on!"

"Do you think she'll go to the cops?" he asks nervously as he puts the car in gear.

I glare at him. "I'm more nervous of what Andrew will do if he catches up to her first."

"Good point." He shudders as we pull away from the curb.

As he rounds our block and starts spiraling outward to encompass a larger search area, I try Karin again. Please, baby, sweetheart, love, pick up.

Nothing.

"Is she really pregnant? Or were you trying to get my sympathy?" His voice is a mix of curious and nervous.

"Yes, she is pregnant. Keep your fucking eyes on the road and don't distract us." I want to punch him again but need to focus on finding Karin—and intercepting Andrew before he gets to her.

Crowds are thin in the rain; I frantically search, looking for curly blonde hair and a blue dress, without a jacket. My gut churns like a washing machine as I think of her running through these streets in fear, not knowing where to go, not knowing who is after her.

Dale can't keep his damn mouth shut. "Seriously, do you think she'll go to the police?"

"No, I don't. But if she did, we would fucking deserve it. Andrew for wanting her dead for no goddamned reason, you for going along with it, and me for not defending her. From you motherfuckers!" My knuckles whiten as I grip the steering wheel.

He's quiet as he drives, both of us looking around. Finally, he says softly, "So ... you think she would have been okay with the business if Drew hadn't threatened her?"

"That is exactly what I am fucking saying. He blew everything. Even if he doesn't take her life, I may never see her again." A blonde in the crowd catches my eye—but no, too tall and long-haired. Damn it.

"Holy shit. Holy shit, James, I'm fucking sorry." He finally gets it.

"You better be."

We keep searching. Every minute or so, I try her phone, praying it isn't out of power and she eventually notices the calls. Baby, please, just pick up.

As we drive and scan the alleyways and sidewalk crowds, I wrestle with regrets. I've had week after week of romancing Karin, but I could never bring myself to tell her the whole story. If I had ...

If I had, we could have talked it over and gotten her settled with the idea well before Andrew learned of her presence. If I had, she could have decided about me without the drama of having a baby. If I had ...

Woulda, coulda, shoulda, I mock myself, my temples throbbing. No point in that now. I made the wrong choice ... and now my lady and my child may have to pay for it.

"I don't get why Drew goes nuts about us dating." Dale is chattering again. I wonder how much pot is in his system. "He didn't talk about security risks when you went to visit your family."

"No, of course not. He doesn't flip out over your stoner buddies either, and I'm sure some shit slips while you're high." I give him an icy look at the next corner and he swallows. "Yeah, thought so. But somehow we're not in jail. And he's not riding your ass about it either. Why? Because he fucking hates either of us being happy with a woman. He's too messed up about women to manage it."

My eyes ache from scanning the streets. Drew's pistol is holstered at my side, and if it comes down to it, I'll stop his bitter ass with a bullet. In fact, I'm tempted to just do it on principle.

"Okay, now I'm mad at the dude," Dale grumbles, and I roll my eyes.

"Now you're mad? He had you pulling a gun on a pregnant woman, and nearly aiding in her murder. He also made you break up with your girlfriend, on even thinner excuses."

"He's sick," Dale growls.

"Yeah, he's mentally ill, but it's not an excuse for much. He abides by his sickness instead of fighting it. He's taking that shit out on the only friends he has and that's only part of his stimulus." I try the phone again, scanning the street with my eyes as I let it ring.

"So what's the rest?" His tone is ridiculously innocent; I want to smack him.

Kid, how did you get into this business? "He hates women. He's convinced himself that every woman in the world is like his ex, who probably isn't half the bitch he describes her as being—she never tried to roll over on him."

I think of my cousin, Terry, who is a miniature, bungling, spineless version of Drew. Terry who apparently is out on bail, and whom I owe a beating as well. Why the fuck do so many men go bonkers about women? Why do they want the rest of us to join—or do they just figure we'll support them?

"I swear to God," I growl. "Even if we get out of this with no one dying or going to jail, I'm done. I can't trust either of you to have my back after the shit you pulled."

His face falls. "Aw man, James, I really am sorry. I didn't know it was gonna be like this!"

"I told you it would happen like this. I told you a few hours ago. You listened to Andrew instead and an innocent pregnant woman may die as a result. Fuck you, Dale." I stare rigidly out the window. Baby, where are you?

"What about the money?" he whines. "You can't just walk away."

"We have enough goddamn money. Also, some things are more significant than others." Now that Karin is in danger, my priorities are crystal clear. "We've picked up twenty million apiece last year alone and I would give every fucking dime away to have her back safely."

He's quiet for a long while as we drive, probing and searching. We've covered ten blocks so far. "She must be hiding somewhere," he verbalizes.

I try the phone again. Nothing.

"Whoa!" The car jolts to a stop and the phone almost flies out of my hands. "I just saw someone jump from the rooftops in that alleyway." He points to the nearest alley.

"What direction?" He gestures. It has to be Andrew. I burst out of the car, shoving the phone in my pocket as I go racing into the alley.

It's possible Andrew has lost her too—he's just searching. Except he wouldn't take to the rooftops unless he wanted to get somewhere fast, on foot. And this means he knows where he's going.

... and that means he somehow knows where she is. Did he slip a tracker in her purse last time he broke in? Or a bug? Is that why he knew what I said and knows where to find her?

It doesn't matter. I'm on him now. Andrew's good at parkour, especially with his gadgets. I'm better—I don't need them.

I jumble up the fire escape and get to the roof. Looking around, I see a figure jumping an alleyway up ahead. He's wearing a familiar dark jacket, and his hair gleams like an ember in the thin daylight.

I bolt for him, leaping the first alleyway and clearing it easily. I don't even break stride as my boots hit the asphalt roof beyond. He's still, and doesn't see me yet; he's preoccupied with peering over the edge of the building with a pair of binoculars.

Then I see him disappear over the edge.

He's found her.

I put everything I have into getting there first.

14

KARIN

Someone keeps buzzing my phone, but I can't stop to look. That red-haired creep may have lost his gun and a tooth or two, but he's on me no matter how fast I run or where I hide. I've barely dodged him twice.

I don't know how he keeps finding me, but it panics me so much, I can barely think. Is it him on the phone, or a frantic James? James. You told me to run while you fought them, and I'm sure you tried your best ... where are you now?

I hear a clang above me—and look up to see the same crazy, woman-hating bastard descending on me, via a fucking rappelling line, with a big hunting knife in his hand. "I've got you, you bitch!"

Thinking quickly, I give him a shove before touches down. He lets out an outraged howl—and smacks against the fire escape; the line gets tangled around the ladder, leaving him awkwardly dangling a foot above the ground. "What?!? Fuck!" he yells, and immediately starts sawing at the tough line with his knife.

Get someplace public; hiding in alleys and building lobbies

isn't working. I bolt for the brightly lit café across the boulevard. What's he going to do, knife me to death in front of a security camera and witnesses?

"I'll fucking kill you, you bitch!" he yells after me hoarsely.

Shit, maybe he will. He's just like my dad and Terry. "Get in line, psycho!" I call back mockingly—as I run as fast as I fucking can. Never let them see you sweat, but never let them get within stabbing range either.

I hear a grunt, the line snapping, and the thud of his boots on the ground. Then I hear him tearing after me. Shit! Shit! Shit ...

A clang sounds high above me and my blood goes cold. His accomplice? I look up—just as James bounds off the alley wall and lands between me and his charging partner.

Oh, thank God.

"Keep running! Get to the café; he won't do shit in front of security cameras!" he calls out as he readies himself for the charging redhead.

I start to obey ... but the bone-jarring thud of them squaring off makes me duck behind a dumpster for cover instead. I poke my head out for a look.

The two are in an all-out brawl. James stands like a wall between my attacker and me, while the other man snarls and lunges and tries to get past him, lashing out with his knife. However, every time he gets too close, he pays for it.

First he nearly loses the knife. He then reels back, holding his face. Then the knife goes clattering across the asphalt.

"Stop defending her, you fucking Judas! She's going to rat us all out!" There's rage in the man's voice—rage, and something else.

Panic.

But he's not the only one who's upset.

"I'll fucking kill you before you touch her!" James' voice shakes with fury and conviction. Again, the guy tries to pass him to get at me, and gets a knee in the gut for his attempt.

"So this is it, huh, Judas?" he pants at James as he staggers back again, holding himself. "You pick some piece of ass over your partners and betray us."

"I haven't betrayed anyone, you stupid bastard; I never even brought you up! You created all of this!" James doesn't just sound angry. There's an incredulous note in his voice, as if he can't believe someone he works with is acting like this.

"I'm not going to jail because of your fucking girlfriend!" the guy roars, eyes wide and spittle gathered at the corners of his mouth.

"Why the fuck did you attack me?" I demand, suddenly enraged as well. I notice a length of broken board leaning against the dumpster and grab it, stepping out. "I didn't even know you exist until you tried to kill me!"

"Shut up, bitch! You know you would have gone to the cops!" He tries for me again, and again James drives him back, this time with a series of hard blows that leave him doubled and staggering. And yet ... he's still trying.

"I told you to run for the café," James admonishes.

"I'm not involving more people in our problems. Besides, he would probably attack me in public." I heft the board and step out.

Inside, I'm terrified, but also pissed, and I reached my limit with bullying, woman-haters a long time ago. And James is here —and he won't let anything bad happen to me.

"What do you think you're gonna do with that, little girl?" Andrew mocks me.

"I think my man and I are going to beat the shit out of you," I reply as I slowly walk forward. James sees the look on my face and smirks, stepping aside for me.

The smirk falls off the other guy's face in incomprehension. "You don't fight back. You run to the cops, like you did with your dad."

"My dad was attacking a twelve-year-old girl a third his size, asshole," I snarl as James and I advance on the guy. He scuttles backward, looking between us nervously. "It's not like I could hit him back.

"And since my personal business is somehow your business, I'll tell you the rest. He beat me from the age of three until I went to the cops to make it stop. Because nobody else intervened and I was too small to defend myself." Anger is replacing my fear fast.

"He went to jail. And because he was obsessed, like you, when he got out, the first thing that he did was try to 'visit' me in my school. With handcuffs, pepper spray, and a knife." I stare at the skinny man in disgust.

"I didn't even call the cops that time. He got into a fight with a security guard. He called them." Why am I explaining all of this?

"And your boyfriend?" he demands. Where did he get all his information? James?

No, he must have done some kind of background check.

"If you're talking about Terry, yeah, I got a restraining order against him. He decided to violate it by trying to kill me. They let him out on bail, which is part of the reason I imposed on James.

"I'm not calling the cops on you because they might tie you to James and I don't want problems because of you. I'm also not calling the cops because they and the legal system are fucking useless when it comes to protecting people."

I take a step toward him and he backs off more. "I don't need them anymore. Not for a crazy, sexist weasel like you."

"I'm not crazy!" he yells, purpling. And he lunges.

James winks at me and gives me room—and I swing the board with all my strength at the blindly charging man.

Bam.

"Good shot!" he calls proudly as the board shatters against the guy's chin and sends him staggering backward.

My fear is gone. Standing there with my arms tingling from the impact, I wonder where it went. But then I see it—in the eyes of my attacker as he holds his bloodied chin and stares at me.

"You got too paranoid, Drew," James says almost sadly. "It's way beyond cautious. And your women issues are fucking up friendships and work. You need to get help."

"How the fuck can you trust her over me? We've known each other for ten years!" he protests, staring at James as he tries to stanch the flow of blood from his nose.

"She's never tried to kill someone I love," he says. "And besides, she's gone through more shit than you, but she's stable, stronger, and kinder. She's also carrying my child, whom you tried to kill along with her."

The confidence in his voice banishes the last of my fright. James, I think, staring at him in awe.

He glances at me, eyebrows rising. "She's pregnant?"

"Yeah. Because you're that far gone, you almost murdered a pregnant woman for no reason. You almost engineered your own arrest by trying to chase her down with a knife. You proud of that, Drew? Is that really who you want to fucking be?" James has his hand near the gun on his belt; I can see it with his jacket pushed aside.

The shock finally gets through to him. He blinks rapidly and shakes his head, as if coming out of a bad dream. "No," he says in a much quieter voice.

In spite of all the fear, drama, and anger, I feel a stab of pity for Andrew, who suddenly has a lost look on his face.

"She wasn't going to say shit to no one. None of this was necessary. It only happened because you let your baggage get the better of you." James' voice is lower now too.

The slow realization of what he's been doing dawn in Andrew's expression. He looks around ... then lowers his hands. "What the fuck do you expect me to do?"

James lets out a bitter laugh and shakes his head. "Leave," he says. "Take your share, take your crap, and leave. You're a multi-millionaire. You can afford a doctor—and a move to another state."

"And if I refuse?" he challenges with his last bit of salt.

"If you ever bother us again, you don't have to worry about what James will do," I say in a steady voice. "I'll shoot you myself."

I don't know if it's bullshit, but it works. He blinks rapidly, then pulls himself upright. "Fair enough," he mutters, wiping the blood off his face.

And he's gone—walking down the alley, hands shoved in his pockets, not even asking for his gun or retrieving his knife. He glances back at us once as he reaches the alley entrance, blends in with the passing crowd, and vanishes.

James huffs a sigh next to me and lowers the gun, turning to me. "I'm so sorry, sweetheart. Are you all right?"

"Um." I drop the broken board and let him gather me into his arms as I cling to him. "No, but I'm getting there. We've ... got a lot to discuss, though."

"Let's go home," he says. "I'll take care of you and make this right, I promise."

I lick my lips, a little nervous about returning to the loft after what happened. "Okay, but I need you to do something to make me feel safer when we get home."

He hugs me tight, kissing the top of my head. "What is it?"

My smile goes a little lopsided. "Grease the balcony and rooftop railings. If that guy tries to break in, I want him to get a nasty surprise."

He lets out a laugh, and cuddles me. "Anything you want, sweetheart."

15

KARIN

"Thanks for helping with the turkey," I tell Samantha as we sit at the loft's timber table. It's Thanksgiving again, and this year, I have a lot more to be thankful for.

"No problem, sis. How's my nephew?" Her voice goes high at the end as she addresses the occupant of the baby seat next to me. He responds by cooing and waving his tiny fists, wide chocolate-brown eyes staring at her in delight.

"Jimmy's fine. He had his three-month checkup last week." Our son is healthy and happy, and we're not doing badly ourselves.

It's been a heck of a year. James actually has started a security company in one of the downstairs offices, which he works at part-time while spending the rest with us. I work out of the loft, half days as well, a handful of clients for now.

Technically, neither of us needs to work; James has more cash than we could spend in our lifetime. But doing so keeps us from getting awkward questions about where the money comes from. And it also means most of that money will be there when we actually retire.

Right now, most of our life is centered on each other, and our son. New Orleans is as beautiful and welcoming as it was a year ago. I haven't been to New York in months; once I testified at Terry's trial, I was done.

Terry got fifteen years for attempted murder, assault with a deadly weapon, simple assault, domestic violence, and repeated violation of a protection order. The whole trial, he and his mother glared at me like I should be on trial. When I testified about the knife, Terry sulked and his mother burst into tears.

I haven't heard from them since the trial.

Now and again, I get some mail forwarded from my old address. Two days ago, it included a card from my mother. Signed, but no note.

I don't know if she's finally realized what my sister and I went through, now that she is trapped in a house with three men who beat up the women they're supposed to love. Maybe, somehow, she's found out she's a grandmother. It could be anything ...but I'm not bothered.

Just because she reaches out doesn't mean I have to respond the way she wants. But I might ... eventually.

If I can forgive someone like Andrew, I would consider giving my mother another chance. She was a coward who didn't defend us ...but she was a victim too.

"Are you guys still okay with my bringing the wife and kids for Christmas?" Samantha asks as she starts passing the salad around.

"Oh yeah, the more the merrier," James says optimistically. He and Samantha have become friends very quickly, which makes me happy. Tentative card-giving or not, she's the only family I have besides my husband and baby.

"Goodie! I want to introduce the kids to their cousin." She sits down on Jimmy's other side and starts making silly faces for him while he squeals and wiggles.

"Hey, could someone pass the butter?" Dale asks at the other end of the table. He's here with his girlfriend, Sherry, a cute Belizean girl with enviable dreadlocks and a bubbly laugh.

It took a while to settle our differences. With work behind them, my husband and his former partner can be friends. As for his pointing a gun at me and my racking him ... we called it even.

James and I have practiced self-defense since I mended from the birth. I've also gone shooting with him. Having him instructing me on protecting myself makes me feel safe even when he's a thousand miles away.

Ironically, Andrew left for Los Angeles a week or so after our confrontation. I must admit—I sighed with relief when I learned he left the state. Dale and James still get emails from him—encrypted, of course.

Apparently he's getting treatment for whatever his ex-wife did to him. I hope it helps—but I'm glad he's gone. His illness may have put the idea of harming me in his head, but he followed it of his own free will.

I can only forgive so much.

"So, what's everyone thankful for this year?" Samantha asks. We didn't even follow this tradition last year, because of Terry and his mother's habitual whining and his father's silence. But this year, things are different. Many things.

"I'm thankful for everything," I say with a smile. My life, my new home, my son, my darling husband, my sister. And most of all, the chance to escape my past and push through to an improved future.

The End.

SIGN UP TO RECEIVE FREE BOOKS

Sign Up to Receive Free E-Books and Audiobook Codes.

Would you like to read **The Unexpected Nanny, Dirty Little Virgin** and **other romance books** for **free?**

You can sign up to receive these free e-books and audiobooks by typing this link into your browser:

https://www.steamyromance.info/free-books-and-audiobooks-hot-and-steamy/

Or this one:

https://www.steamyromance.info/the-unexpected-nanny-free/

PREVIEW OF ON THE RUN

A SECRET BABY ROMANCE

By Michelle Love

Blurb

Murder. Lies. Fraud. Just another day in the lives of billionaires and women on the run.

Mercedes Gravage didn't mean to be present when a girl at a party overdosed, and she certainly didn't expect she would be the one to take the fall for it.
But here she is, on the run and in need of a place to stay. She needs a new identity, and she's found one as a nanny.
Kane Stockwell is fighting with life. He's fighting with his ex-wife, who ran off with his business partner, and he's fighting to keep his company from succumbing to accusations of fraud. He knows that he's going to have to figure out something soon, or things are going to get even harder.
Little does he know that the girl he hired to take care of his son

is about to change his life—in more ways than he ever imagined. She's captivating, completely mesmerizing. But there's a lot Kane doesn't know about Mercedes—including the fact that she's a virgin.

When life crumbles around them and their happiness is threatened to the core, can Kane keep it all together, or have the authorities finally caught up with Mercedes?

Kane Stockwell

I'm a billionaire. I don't ask for anything in life. If I want it, I get it.

I've got most women begging for my attention, and I don't even have the time of day for them. Of course, life would be easier if I wasn't fighting my ex-wife and ex-business partner, the two people I trusted most in the world who stabbed me in the back. I have to take care of my son now. I have to focus on the empire I'm building for him one day.

Then I meet this girl.

She tells me her name is Emily, and she loves working with children. She's perfect for my son, but what is she doing to me?

She's been on my mind since the day I hired her. I can't stop her body from ruling my thoughts. I have to have her. I have to show her what it's like to have a real man between her sheets.

It's been months—years, even—since I've desired a woman so powerfully.

I will have her.

She's in my sights; it's only a matter of time.

Mercedes Gravage

I'm the girl who has it all. Good grades, full scholarship, good looks, charm.

I know that if I want something bad enough, I can get it.
Was any of it handed to me? Of course not. I have clawed my way to the top, and I intend to stay there.
Until I'm accused of a crime that I didn't commit.
Forced to go on the run, I know that I'm going to have to figure out how this happened and soon. I can't end up in prison for the rest of my life. I've got to lay low.
But then I meet Kane Stockwell.
He is the man of my dreams. Of course, I didn't know this before I met him, but he's everything I've ever wanted. And I know he wants me too. I'll work for him, I'll take care of his son, but I'll want him every time I see him.
He can't know the truth about me. He can't find out my secret. If he does, he'll turn me in.
I've got to lay low.

But how long can I keep this up?

CHAPTER 1

"And how does the jury find Miss Gravage?"

My heart races as I look from one face to the next, noting that none of the men or women in the jury stand will meet my gaze. There is silence in the courtroom for only a brief moment, then one man in the corner of the box rises, clearing his throat and looking at me with a stone-cold stare.

"Your Honor, the members of this jury have found Miss Gravage to be guilty of deliberate homicide, and we recommend she be punished to the fullest extent of the law."

My heart races, and I return my gaze to the judge. He sits silently for a moment, then he smacks the gavel on his desk and lays down the punishment. "Miss Gravage, you have been found guilty of the murder of Miss Amanda Hamilton and shall serve a sentence of life behind bars—without parole. Dismissed!"

He hits the desk again, and a police officer comes forward. I'm screaming and crying, proclaiming my innocence, but no one's listening to me. They drag me out of the courtroom in my orange jumpsuit and handcuffs, then push me into the back of a cop car. There are reporters everywhere, each one thrusting a microphone in my face.

The next thing I know I'm being shoved into a cold, dark jail cell. There is a metal cot without a blanket or a pillow, a toilet in the corner, and the entire thing is made out of dreary, gray concrete. The bars slam closed behind me, and I fall to my knees, screaming as the sound of the guard's boots retreat into the darkness.

I shoot up in bed, crying out and thrashing in my sheets. My chest is heaving, and I look around the cheap hotel room, awareness coming back to me in waves. I slowly remember where I am. I'm not in court. I'm not in jail. I've seen both during my teenage years, but never for anything as serious as murder.

Why do I think I'm going to jail?

Oh yeah. Amanda Hamilton.

Amanda Hamilton was a girl I'd known for only a few days before my whole life went to shit. She was a member of a rival sorority and was one of those people who felt the world owed her something. That I owed her something. I had to admit, she was a beautiful girl, but no more beautiful than me or countless other women.

So after I'd set my sights on Jordan Stone, I wasn't going to just let her move on him without putting up a fight.

Why should she get first dibs on a boy just because she had seniority over me at the school? It was clear that he thought I was attractive, and we hit it off immediately. When he asked me out to several parties on campus, I knew that he felt something between us too. I'd even entertained thoughts that he might be the man I would lose my virginity to. He might have even been the man I would marry one day. In short, I was head over heels in love with him.

But so was Amanda.

I was so stupid, thinking that when she invited me to a party at her sorority, it was because she wanted to get to know me. She and her friends were all cut from the same cloth, and worse yet, none of them were very smart. When word spread that she had overdosed on whatever drug they had managed to get their hands on, I can't say that I was surprised.

What did surprise me, however, was the rumor spreading around campus the next day that I'd had something to do with her overdose. Sure, I had no love for the girl, and she wasn't a fan of me either, but I wasn't a killer, and I never could be. I've never wanted anyone dead, not even my worst enemy.

But I soon learned that rumors spread just as quickly in college as they do in high school, and once the nasty story took root, I was done for. I knew that the police were ruling the overdose an accident for the moment, but I didn't want to be around when they changed their mind. I had no doubt that they were going to get wind of the gossip that I'd had something to do with it, and once that happened, I was in deep.

I already have a record. And that record shows drugs and incarceration in my past. It was only high school stupidity because I wanted to be one of the cool kids, but it almost cost me my scholarship to the University of California San Diego. I learned my lesson, and I swore off drugs forever. I would never touch the stuff again, but here they are again, ruining my life once more.

With a sigh, I throw the sheets off my body and swing my legs to the floor. I'm thinking more clearly now about what happened and about what I'm going to do. That is, what I am doing. I'm on the run. I wasn't about to hang around and take the fall for that dummy's mistake, that's for damn sure. I don't know where I'm going or what I'm going to do when I get there, but I know I can't stay in California.

I grab my purse and pull out my wallet, flipping through the little bit of cash I have left. I jumped on the first available flight out of the state, and now, a few days later, I'm sitting in the cheapest hotel in Chicago. It's a city I've been in before, but I don't remember it being so dreary.

Sitting on the bed, I check my phone. I scroll through a variety of text messages from friends wondering where I am, but naturally, I see nothing from either of my parents. Surely by now they would know that their daughter is allegedly missing, but neither of them care enough to reach out to me.

I'm not going to answer any of the text messages anyway. It's just a matter of time before I ditch this phone. What I need is a way to make money and fast. I don't know if I'm going to stay in Chicago, but by the looks of my wallet, this is going to be my home for a while. I pull up a job-posting website on my phone and scroll through the postings, searching for anything that looks easy and as unofficial as possible. I don't want to go through a lengthy interview process. I can't.

The last thing I want to do is draw any more attention to myself than necessary. If I do, I'm cooked.

A listing catches my eye:

Looking for a New Nanny ASAP

Unfortunately, I find myself once again looking for a nanny for my young son. He's a spirited boy who needs someone who understands him. I need a live-in to care for him around the clock as my work keeps me out of the home. I need someone who is able to meet his needs.

I've tried using agencies, but their nannies seem completely unable to do their jobs. I need someone capable. Please respond with an e-mail about yourself. Include your name, phone number, and experience, and I will get back to you if I think you may be a good fit.

Be thorough and follow the directions. Any applicants who do not will be discarded. Thank you.

Kane Stockwell

I stare at the posting, my heart racing. It's only a few hours old, and it's absolutely perfect for me. I quickly send him an e-mail, careful to describe myself in the best possible terms and to follow his directions. The only thing I change is my name. I might be Mercedes Gravage, but if he watches the news at all then it won't be long before knows who that is.

My new name is Emily Rhodes. It's both common enough, yet unique. He shouldn't question it. I don't have a lot of experience with children, but they're children. How hard can they be? Everyone has kids. And if everyone can do it, then *anyone* can do it—and I'm anyone.

I set my phone aside, and I'm surprised when I get a text almost immediately. It's from a number I don't know, but the sender immediately identifies himself as Kane.

Hello, and thank you for your application. I would like to conduct an interview with you as soon as possible. Can you come in today?

My heart races as I stare at the text. This is too good to be true. I smile to myself as I quickly send him a reply:

Thanks for getting back to me. I would love to meet you—just say when and where.

I hit Send and lay back on the bed with a smile. This is too perfect.

This is the solution to my problems.

CHAPTER 2

"Mr. Stockwell, I imagine if you are on your phone, then it must be something pretty damn important. If you don't want to share it with the rest of the group, I'll thank you to stay off of it until this meeting is over." Mr. Trist put his fists on the table, leaning forward and fixing me with his no-nonsense glare.

Annoyed, I set my phone down on the table and clasped my hands in front of me, elbows on the table. "Apologies, gentlemen, but I have a young son at home, and he needs care. My latest nanny bailed on me at the last second, and I've been scrambling to find another."

"That's all well and good, but we're trying to run a company here. If you want the money to pay that nanny, you need to be present here, and I don't just mean filling that chair. Give us the rundown on what you see for next quarter," Mr. Trist continued.

I rise from my chair, masking my annoyance. I hate these meetings, and I hate dealing with my investors. I know it's not a good idea to hate those who fund business, but I despise how they act like this is their company, their idea. I started Star Enterprises, and I'm the sole owner.

Their shares mean nothing save for the fact that they get profit. Relieved that I've secured another babysitter so quickly, I walk over to the chart on the wall and start pointing out figures to the men at the table. As I give the presentation, I see the my phone blinking.

I've either received another text or missed a call, and I don't have the time to get to it right now. I can feel the aggravation creeping into the back of my mind, but one word to any of the shareholders about this, and it would be as good as throwing myself to the wolves. I'm in enough legal trouble already; I don't want to raise suspicion with them that there's anything wrong with the company.

At long last, I finish the presentation and call an end to the meeting.

"As always, I look forward to seeing you all again," I lie as they start for the door. I shake hands warmly with each of the six men, keenly aware that each would just as soon stab me in the back than be at this meeting. When the last of them has finally left, I hurry over and grab my phone.

I'm hoping it's the new nanny confirming that she can come to the house later on this afternoon.

It's not.

It's a missed call from Cheryl, my ex-wife. Rage builds in my chest as I raise the phone to my ear, and I cringe as I hear her voice.

"Kane, how nice of you to be avoiding my calls after all I've done for you! I'm getting sick and tired of your bullshit! You better get this straightened out or there's going to be hell to pay. Of course, you know how you can make this all go away! Blake and I would be most interested in hearing how you pulled off a few of those big trades that you managed back in the day. Care to share? Ta!" The automated voice signaled the end of my messages, and I nearly slammed my phone back down on the table. I was sick and tired of dealing with that woman, and I wanted her out of my life forever.

When she and I had first met, it had been fireworks. I thought she was the most perfect woman on the planet, and I wanted to spend the rest of my life with her. She hadn't been there from day one like Blake Harper, my business partner, but I'd wanted her there for every day thereafter.

What an idiot I'd been for her.

Back in college I had managed to land a few major stock trades. I found out a way to get around the normal algorithm, and I had made billions off the deals. It had been Blake's idea to start the company, helping those who wanted to do the same.

Of course, I never shared my real secrets with the public, which was why I was facing certain legal issues now. We promised that anyone in the world could make millions, and that just wasn't happening. And the customers were noticing.

To add insult to injury, just as the legal bills started piling up, I caught Blake in bed with my wife. The two eventually got together, Cheryl leaving me and every part of the life we'd made together behind, including our son.

My boy had been devastated when she left, but it had devastated me even more. Not only did I lose my wife and the mother of my child, but I'd also lost my business partner.

Up until recently, she hadn't had any interest in seeing little Troy. I'd made promise after promise to him that he would see her soon, but she never showed. Eventually, I decided enough was enough and got full custody of him—at least for now. But only a couple months ago, Cheryl started coming around again. My guess is she ran out of money and wants more.

But that's not going to happen. I'm not going to give some bitch who abandonned her family an allowance. If she wants money, she can get a job. Or she can go crying to Blake. He seemed to be her knight in shining armor a year ago, so what the hell is he doing now?

I sigh as I sit back down in my chair, more agitated than I was during the meeting. I light a cigarette and put it to my lips, taking a long drag before exhaling slowly.

"Oh, sir, it's you. I was about to tell whoever was in here that you don't like smoking in the building, but I'll take my leave." Missy Jarvis, my secretary, started to pull her head back out of the conference room, but I stop her.

"Come in here for a second, Missy" I ask. As she walks closer to my seat, I see her slight cringe at the smell of the cigarette.

"Yes, sir?" she asks meekly. She may be expecting more work dumped on her, but I don't want to take on anything else right now either. I have other things to do with my day.

"I'm going to be leaving early today, and I want you to make sure that the boys on the floor get through the list I put up this morning. They all got it in their e-mails, so make sure that they actually get through it. Any shithead who says he didn't receive gets to stay late until it's done, understood?" I ask. She smiles and nods, and then glances down at the files in her hands.

"Did you have any more luck finding a nanny for Troy?" she asks. On the surface, it appears to be sincere, but I know there's more to it than a friendly inquiry. I know she wants to sleep with me. It's been written on her face since the day I hired her. Lately, she's taken a special interest in my son, and I get the impression it's because she's trying to get on my good side.

"As a matter of fact, that's why I'm leaving early. I have someone coming to the house in an hour, so I need to get going," I reply. I take another drag of the cigarette before stubbing it out on the table. I throw it in the garbage and nod over my shoulder. "Be a doll and wipe that up for me."

"Yes, sir," she says as she steps forward to brush it into her hand. I don't bother to tell her that her hands are going to stink of cigarette for the rest of the day. Perhaps that's what she wants. Perhaps it reminds her of me. I walk out of the room and avoid eye contact with the other employees as I stalk through the hall and step into the elevator.

I've got to get back to my house. Without a nanny looking after things the past couple of days, I have to get a few things straightened up before this new girl arrives.

And I need time to pick up Troy from daycare.

CHAPTER 3

I open my eyes, the sound of my alarm on the nightstand beside me waking me up. It's the first time I've slept all the way through the night since going on the run, and I feel remarkably refreshed. Switching it off, I head to the bathroom, glad I gave myself some extra time to get ready before the kid would be getting up.

I'm startled once more when I look at my reflection in the mirror. The long brunette hair that I've sported for most of my life has been replaced by a short blonde bob. Anything to help hide my identity, I would do gladly. I got it done the morning of my interview, so Mr. Stockwell has no idea what my natural color is.

I couldn't believe how quickly he gave me the job. He hardly asked any questions, and accepted the name Emily as though it was my real name. But then, of course he thought it was. Why wouldn't he?

After applying some light makeup and tieing my hair back, I slip into jeans and a T-shirt. Mr. Stockwell instructed me to dress comfortably for my shifts as I'll likely be spending most of my time chasing Troy around and doing some light cleaning. So far, three days in, things have been going very well, but I know I have to do a better job when it comes to talking to Kane.

Kane Stockwell is by far the most gorgeous man I have ever seen in my life. He is tall, handsome, muscular, and has piercing blue eyes. I've only seen him dressed in his professional work suit, but I can clearly see the outlines of what lies underneath. I thought that I'd been attracted to that boy back in college, but I'm seeing now what a real man looks like.

Not to mention, it's obvious that he truly loves his son. Everything in the house revolves around that kid. I don't mind it. My room is right across the hall from his son, and it's utter luxury. I vaguely remember a family trip to Vegas when I was small, and this mansion is even better than the five-star hotel we'd stayed in.

I hear the sound of the front door opening and closing, and I know Kane has left for work. Though I would have liked to see him, I have to admit, I'm grateful to start my morning without making a fool of myself. I don't know what I'm going to say to him the next time I see him, but I'm determined it's going to be something that sounds smart. I feel like a idiot every time I try to talk to him, and it's embarrassing.

"Miss Emily! Miss Emily, I'm hungry! Feed me!" Troy's voice echoes through the hall, and I quickly finish adjusting my clothing.

"Wow, you're up early. I thought you were going to sleep in, you little monkey," I say with a smile as I walk out into the hall. "I'm going to get your breakfast in just a sec. Why don't you put some real clothes on?"

"No! I want food now! I'm starving!" Troy shoots back.

"I'm sure it's not all that bad. I'm going to get you some food, okay? I've just got to—" I start, but the boy bursts into tears and collapses in the middle of the hallway.

"I'm starving! Feed me!" he wails. The sound of his sobs is

deafening, and I take a deep breath. I can already understand why so many nannies have given up on this job. If the pay wasn't so nice, I'd be happily cleaning hotels for cash under the table instead of this.

"Troy, we aren't going to act like this. I told you that I'm going to make you breakfast, but I want you to get dressed," I say in the calmest tone I can muster. I want to shove him right back into his bedroom and tell him to stop having a fit, but I know that's not going to get me anywhere. He's clearly used to getting his own way, and when that doesn't happen, he throws a fit.

The boy has had no discipline in his life.

"No! I told you to get me food, and I mean get it now!" he screams once more as he throws his bear at me. It connects with my face despite the fact that I tried to dodge it, and I cry out. Its hard little nose hit me right in the eye. I feel anger rising in my chest, and I know that I can't lose my temper, but I'm beginning to regard this kid as a little brat.

He's in a heap on the floor sobbing, and I'm about to reprimand him for throwing toys when a voice startles me from behind. "What's going on here?"

I whirl around. Kane is standing at the top of the staircase, staring at both of us with a blank face. I wish there was something in his expression to give away his thoughts about witnessing this scene, but he doesn't show a thing. I can't tell if he's angry, surprised, or simply used to this kind of behavior. He looks first at his son, then back at me, and it seems that as soon as Troy notices his father standing in the hall, he gets even louder.

"She won't feed me, Daddy! I asked her so nice if she would make me breakfast, and she told me she's not going to!" Troy sobs. My anger simmers a little hotter, but Kane and I have at least one thing in common—I'm good at hiding my emotions too.

"Nothing is going on, we've just gotten off to a bit of a rough start this morning," I say, ignoring Troy.

"She *never* makes me food when I ask! I get so hungry!" Troy sobs once more. He picks himself up off the floor and theatrically lurches over to the wall. I hear him slump against his door, and I fight the urge to roll my eyes. I've seen some dramatic children in my life, but nothing quite this bad.

Kane looks at his son once more, then back at me. There is a silence in the hallway now that is almost deafening, and everything inside me screams to explain the situation.

But nothing comes to mind. I can't tell this father right in front of his child that the boy is being unreasonable. Troy is nearly six years old. He's plenty old enough to tell the truth, but he's also old enough to tell a lie. I'm not sure what his father thinks of any of this, and I wish he would say something that would clue me in.

Kane merely gives a nod and turns and walks up the hall. He's heading for his bedroom, and I'm not sure what he's doing. I know better than to follow him or ask, so I turn around and give Troy a look. Though Troy is very young, I swear that I see a smirk on his face. I want nothing more than to put him on his bed and tell him he's taking a time-out, but I don't dare.

If he threw that big of a fit because he didn't get his breakfast right away, I can't imagine the scene he'd cause if I touched him. I decide that it's better to go make him breakfast, and forget about the entire morning. After all, the last thing I want to do is make it look like I can't handle a child.

I hear the sound of Kane's footsteps on the hardwood floor as I pour some cereal in a bowl, and I take a deep breath. I'm prepared to hear him lecture me not to let that happen again. I'm sure he's not happy about coming home to such a fit, or about having to wonder whether his new nanny is even able to take care of his son.

But, he says nothing about the incident. As he walks through the kitchen, he gives me another nod without a smile. "I hope you have a good day."

"You too!" I call after him, a little more enthusiastically than I mean to. I stand with my eyes closed, kicking myself for being so awkward, and I hear the sound of the door opening and closing again.

As the boy takes his seat at the kitchen table, I toss the food in front of him and say nothing. I don't care if I make friends with the kid or not. I'm not in the mood to cater to someone who is impossible to please.

Besides, I'm his nanny, not his friend. If the boy needs to learn some lessons, then I'm supposed to be the one to do that.

I walk to the window next to the backdoor and look out, watching as Kane's Jaguar pulls out of the drive and into the street, speeding off toward downtown. I sigh. I want so badly to make a good impression on him, and it couldn't have gone much worse that morning. I've got to get the hang of this.

I've got to prove to him that I can do it.

My life—or my safety, at the very least—depends on it.

CHAPTER 4

"Look, Cheryl, I get what you're saying, and I know you're pissed about this, but I'm not going to change my mind. You're the one who walked out on *us*. I didn't tell you to fuck my best friend, and I didn't tell you to run off with him either. Troy doesn't care if you're around or not anymore. You've hurt him too many times for him to give a damn what you're doing!" I didn't want to reach the point of screaming, but here I am, shouting into my phone as I sit in my car after a long day at the office.

"That child will believe whatever bullshit you feed him, and I'm not going to stand for it. Troy is just as much my son as he is yours, and you're going to start letting me see him, or you're going to be sorry!" Cheryl snaps back.

"What're you going to do, ignore us to death? Why don't you do the world a favor and run off to that Caribbean bungalow you're always talking about? I think we could all use another one of your little disappearing acts!" I snidely reply.

"You would like that, wouldn't you? All your problems just conveniently disappear? Well guess what, it's only a matter of time before I see you in court, and you've got another thing coming. I wasted enough of my life letting you push me around, and I'm not going to let you do that to me anymore! Do you understand? It's over for you!" She doesn't give me the chance to reply, and I want to throw my phone in the back seat when I hear the line cut off.

I slam my hands against the steering wheel, angrier than I've been in a long while. It's been difficult for us to have contact with each other—it never ends well—and I'm getting sick of it. I already dread answering the phone when I see her name, and it's only getting worse.

Thankfully, at this point Blake has the sense to avoid talking to me. I don't know what he plans to say when he does, but I'm sure that it's coming. He was enough of my equal in the company that I'm sure he's going to come knocking at one point or another, especially if he's got Cheryl barking at him.

I remember what it was like to be married to that woman, and though I have to admit that it was invigorating at first, toward the end it was my worst nightmare. I shake my head and hit the steering wheel again before starting the engine and pulling out of the parking lot.

When I pull into my driveway, I glance at the windows and sigh. I don't want to go in there and make small talk. I don't want to answer questions about what I want for dinner, because the fact of the matter is, I don't even know. But I know that I can't sit in my car forever, so I drag myself out from behind the wheel and start for the house.

I open the door, dreading the inevitable sound of screaming and all the tales my son has from the day. I know most of them are exaggerated, but there has to be at least a little bit of truth to them, I think. I don't want him to be unhappy, and I really don't want to lose another nanny. I can't deal with that right now. Not on top of everything else.

I hear soft music playing when I crack open the door, and

curious, I push it open the rest of the way. I walk inside and immediately see Emily cooking dinner. She looks over her shoulder and smiles at me with Troy beside her, using a butter knife to slice strawberries and bananas into a bowl.

"Daddy! Lookie Daddy! Miss Emily is letting me help her in the kitchen! Lookie at me!" he beams, and I walk over to him with a smile on my face. It's good to come home to a peaceful house, and I'm happy that he's having a good time.

"What? Since when are you old enough to use a knife? Are you sure you're big enough for that?" I ask in a teasing voice. I wrap my arms around him and plant a kiss on his cheek, and he smiles the biggest smile I've seen in a while.

The past few days have really changed my son for the better. I've been noticing more and more that he really likes Emily, which makes my life so much easier. I can only hope this lasts, but I know better than to get attached to any nanny.

"I am big enough. Emily said that this knife is perfect for fruit and she wants me to do it!" He smiles over at her, and she smiles back, though her eyes quickly return to the pan of simmering hamburger in front of her.

"I thought that he might like to give me a hand in the kitchen. It seemed like a better option than another episode of that show he watches." She gives me a warm smile, and I nod.

"I appreciate you letting him help you and thank you for getting dinner going too. Wow, I have to say, this place looks amazing. When did you have the time to get it all cleaned up and take care of this little monster, too?" I ruffle Troy's mop of hair and look around the house in amazement. Not only has she gotten dinner on, but I can see that she's vacuumed, dusted, and that there's a variety of Troy's clean clothes folded neatly in a basket.

"I'm not quite done yet. I wanted to finish the laundry and take care of the pantry, but that's going to have to wait until tomorrow. You don't mind if I get rid of the food that's expired, do you? I noticed earlier when I was picking out dinner that there are a few things that are past their prime." She smiles at me once more, and I quickly shake my head.

"If there is anything you think needs to be tossed, toss it. I hate to have you do all this when you're watching Troy, too, but I do appreciate it. Perhaps we'll need to discuss a pay raise." I see her eyes light up at the prospect, but she says nothing.

"I'm going to make a grocery list and get a few things tomorrow. I thought Troy might like a little surprise outing. Perhaps we'll stop and get ice cream on the way home, but only if he's a good boy." She gives my son a look, and for the first time I've ever seen in my life, he is quick to assure her he's going to be.

"I'll be good! I want a chocolate cone! I want chocolate ice cream!" he shouts, and she puts her finger to her lips.

"Shhh, remember what we talked about? You have to use your indoor voice when we're inside the house, then you can use your outdoor voice when you're outside. What kind of cone would you like?" She puts her hands on her hips and looks at him with a stern but gentle look, and once again I hardly recognize my son.

He lowers his voice immediately and returns his attention to the banana in front of him as he replies, "I want a chocolate cone, please."

"Then you shall have a chocolate cone," Emily responds with a smile. She turns to me and motions for me to head upstairs. "I've almost got the rest of the taco fixings done, and I think Troy is about done with the fruit salad there. You better get ready for dinner if you want it while it's hot."

"I can't remember the last time we had tacos," I say with a shake of my head. "I'll be right back."

I turn and head up the stairs, my mind still spinning. She made tacos. I really can't remember the last time I had a taco, and it sounds delicious. All the nannies I'd hired from the agency were always making some delicacy for dinner. I was never sure if they were told that they had to do that, or if they did it to impress me, but Troy rarely liked what was on the table in front of him. I felt that was part of the problem with him and his nannies. They were never paying attention to what he wanted or needed, but rather spent too much time doing what they thought I wanted.

All I wanted was for them to keep my son happy—and well-behaved.

So far, Emily's had a profound effect on him, and I can't explain that either. One day he's screaming at her in the hall, then barely a week later I come home, and he's like a different child. It's such a nice change from what I'm used to, I can hardly believe it.

As I change my clothes into something more casual for dinner, I think about Cheryl once more. She can bitch about the way things are all she wants, but I can see that my son is happy now, and I'm not going to do anything—or allow her to do anything—to risk that.

She made her choice, and I've made mine. I can live with life like this. In fact, I like my life like this. Whether Cheryl's happy with her life and the choices she's made is not my problem.

I am happy again, finally.

CHAPTER 5

"Alright Mercedes, you've got this. All you have to do is grab a few things at the store, then take the kid to get ice cream. You'll be home in less than an hour, and you can go back to hiding." I put thick, round sunglasses on, covering most of my face. I follow it with an exaggerated sun hat, hoping that my look isn't so out there that Troy points it out.

Finishing it off with bright red lipstick—something I never wore at college—I walk out of my bathroom and peek into his room. "Are you ready?"

"Yes, Miss Emily!" Troy says as he quickly gets up from playing with his toys on the floor. I'm finally getting used to him calling me Emily. For a while, it was hard not to correct him and tell him my real name. But I was careful to break that habit as soon as possible. The last thing I want is to slip up and come out with the truth.

"You look adorable in that shirt," I say as the two of us leave the house. He nods and heads directly for the car, but I stop him. It's the one thing I hadn't thought about before we left the house, and I suddenly realize that I should avoid driving as much as possible.

"Daddy said that we could take his car today," Troy says as he hangs off the handle of the car door. I can hear the tension in his voice, and I know that I have to be careful if I want to keep him from throwing a fit—which I do. I will do anything to keep him from melting down in public, but I can't risk getting pulled over and having to show my ID to a cop.

"I know he did, but like I told him this morning, I thought that the weather was perfect for a walk! Don't you want to get some fresh air?" I ask with a smile. He gives me a look that tells me he would rather do anything than walk with me, but I ignore it.

"I want to ride in Daddy's car! He doesn't let me much, and it's a fancy car! I want to ride in it!" Troy shouts. I give him a warning look and put my fingers to my lips.

"What did I tell you about—" I start, but he cuts me off.

"We're outside! I can use my outside voice if I want!" he shouts again.

"Okay, I know that we're outside, but using your outside voice and shouting at me are two different things. You still have to be nice, even when you're talking louder outside." I cross my arms and look at him, and he throws himself to the ground. I brace myself for him to start crying about a scratched arm or skinned knee, and I'm happy when he doesn't.

"I thought you wanted to go get ice cream," I try again, this time using a different angle.

"I do! I want a chocolate ice cream cone!" he snaps at me. I'm thankful he keeps his voice lower this time.

"Well then, let's go. You aren't going to get much of an ice cream cone if you stay here in the driveway," I say with a laugh. I can see he doesn't know what to make of me, and I wonder how many nannies in the past have simply given in to his demands once he started throwing a big enough fit.

I walk through the gate, and leaving it open, I start walking away up the sidewalk. In the back of my mind, I wonder how far I can go before I should turn around and make sure he's coming with me, and it's not until I'm on the very brink of turning around that I hear his little feet on the pavement, running to catch up.

"There you are! I thought I was going to have to get ice cream all on my own," I say with a smile. He's pouting, but he's coming, and that's all I care about. We walk side by side in silence for a few seconds, and then I offer him my hand. "You know, I would love to hold the hand of a handsome boy like you as we walk down the street."

"I don't want to hold your hand!" he snips at me. I pull my hand back and sigh.

"Alright then, if you don't want to be my best friend, you don't have to be," I look the other way, but I can tell I've got his attention now.

"I don't have a best friend," he says at last. "But I want one. I don't get one because I don't go to daycare or school. I didn't like the kids at daycare, either. They weren't very nice."

I glance down at him, suddenly finding a new level of compassion for him. His dad did mention that he had to take Troy to daycare for a few days while he looked for another nanny, but I didn't think about how hard that could be on the kid. Sure, going to someone else's house when he was used to living in his own had to be tough, but I didn't think about how the other kids would have treated him.

"You know, when I went to school people weren't very nice to me, either. I'm glad that I met a nice boy like you," I say with a smile. He looks up at me with another smile, and to my surprise, he puts his hand in mine. I feel a thrill rush through my heart. I'm breaking through to this little boy, and no nanny has been able to do that before. I'm making an impression on him, and that makes my heart tug in a way I never would've expected.

There have been a lot of things about this job that I didn't expect, not least of which is the impression that one gruff, quiet Daddy has had on me.

Kane is the one person who's been on my mind even more than Amanda the past week, and I don't know what to do with my thoughts. I know he's stressed at work, though I'm not entirely sure what it is he's stressed about. He doesn't tell me much, and I don't ask. All I know is that he's paying me to be the nanny, and that's it.

But from what I can tell, he's having issues with his ex-wife. Of course, I can't deny that knowing that there's an issue between the two of them makes me happy. I can't stop fantasizing about Kane, and I don't feel so guilty about it, knowing that he doesn't have a woman in his life.

In my deepest desires, I want to be the one he looks forward to coming home to see, even if I am the nanny. I can play wife as best I can, even if I do have to keep it professional. It's a harmless game to play in my head, so long as he doesn't find out about it.

And as long as he doesn't figure out who I am, I can keep this up for a very long time.

And boy, have I been taking precautions. I know he likes to watch the news in the morning, but I'm always careful to turn off the TV and talk to him about something relating to my duties when any story about me comes on. At first, I was afraid that he was going to figure it out, but he's always so caught up in his work that he doesn't seem to care at all.

The less he hears about the story, the better. The only problem is, that means I don't get to learn anything new about the story either. I don't have the time to go looking for what they're saying about it during the day, and I don't dare keep it on with anyone around.

I don't know if they're looking for me or how close they are to finding me. I want to believe that they have let me go, but in the back of my mind, I can't stop thinking about that recurring dream.

I grip Troy's hand a little tighter, and we pick up the pace.

"Ow! Why are we hurrying?" he asks, clearly annoyed.

"I just think we should get the shopping done quickly. I want to have that ice cream," I say with a smile. He seems satisfied with my answer, but I can't shake the paranoid feeling that's overtaken me. I want to get through these errands, and I want to get home as soon as possible.

I already avoid answering the door or the house phone as much as possible. Going out in public is having an even worse effect on my nerves. I take a deep breath and let it out again as we cross the street directly in front of a police car.

They don't know who you are, Mercedes. Just get the groceries and get out. You don't even have to take off your glasses. You'll be fine. Just fine.

The thoughts run through my mind, and I try to focus on the moment. I tell myself I'm going to be fine, but there's an unshakeable feeling in my heart that I'm on borrowed time. As much as I've come to enjoy working for Kane and Troy and wish this could be my life forever, I fear that it's not going to happen.

It's just a matter of time before they catch me, and once they do, I'm worried I'll go to jail for a crime that I didn't commit.

If you want to continue reading this story, you can get your copy from your favorite vendor by searching for the title:

On the Run
A Secret Baby Romance

You can also find the e-book version by typing this link in your computer's browser:

https://www.hotandsteamyromance.com/products/on-the-run-a-secret-baby-romance

OTHER BOOKS BY THIS AUTHOR

Saving Her Rescuer: A Billionaire & A Virgin Romance

I WAS JUST TRYING to get away from my crazy ex for the weekend when I ended up in a giant pileup on the highway up to Gore Mountain.

HTTPS://GENI.US/SAVINGHERRESCUER

∽

Sensual Sounds: A Rockstar Ménage

Lust. Lies. Double lives.

. . .

THE ROCK and roll industry is full of people who are looking out for themselves and willing to do anything to rise to the top.

HTTPS://WWW.HOTANDSTEAMYROMANCE.COM/COLLECTIONS/
FRONTPAGE/PRODUCTS/SENSUAL-SOUNDS-A-ROCKSTAR-MENAGE

∾

ON THE RUN: A Secret Baby Romance

MURDER. Lies. Fraud. Just another day in the lives of billionaires and women on the run.

HTTPS://WWW.HOTANDSTEAMYROMANCE.COM/COLLECTIONS/
FRONTPAGE/PRODUCTS/ON-THE-RUN-A-SECRET-BABY-ROMANCE

∾

THE DIRTY DOCTOR'S TOUCH: A Billionaire Doctor Romance

I AM A MASTER. An elitist. I am at the top of my field, and I know what I am doing.

HTTPS://WWW.HOTANDSTEAMYROMANCE.COM/COLLECTIONS/
FRONTPAGE/PRODUCTS/THE-DIRTY-DOCTOR-S-TOUCH-A-
BILLIONAIRE-DOCTOR-ROMANCE

THE HERO SHE NEEDS: A Single Daddy Next Door Romance

HE'S the only man I've ever wanted...

HTTPS://WWW.HOTANDSTEAMYROMANCE.COM/COLLECTIONS/FRONTPAGE/PRODUCTS/THE-HERO-SHE-NEEDS-A-SINGLE-DADDY-NEXT-DOOR-ROMANCE

YOU CAN FIND all of my books here

HOT AND STEAMY Romance
https://www.hotandsteamyromance.com

ABOUT THE AUTHOR

Mrs. Love writes about smart, sexy women and the hot alpha billionaires who love them. She has found her own happily ever after with her dream husband and adorable 6 and 2 year old kids.

Currently, Michelle is hard at work on the next book in the series, and trying to stay off the Internet.

"Thank you for supporting an indie author. Anything you can do, whether it be writing a review, or even simply telling a fellow reader that you enjoyed this. Thanks

 facebook.com/HotAndSteamyRomance
 instagram.com/michellesromance

©Copyright 2020 by Michelle Love - All rights Reserved
In no way is it legal to reproduce, duplicate, or transmit any part of this document in either electronic means or in printed format. Recording of this publication is strictly prohibited and any storage of this document is not allowed unless with written permission from the publisher. All rights are reserved.
Respective authors own all copyrights not held by the publisher.

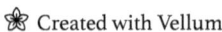 Created with Vellum

www.ingramcontent.com/pod-product-compliance
Lightning Source LLC
LaVergne TN
LVHW021717060526
838200LV00050B/2723